The Freedom Ballet

notionpress.com

The Freedom Ballet

Balram Chand

notionpress.com

Notion Press

5 Muthu Kalathy Street, Triplicane,

Chennai - 600 005

First Published by Notion Press 2015

ISBN: 978-93-52060-41-2

I dedicate this book to my wonderful wife and to my daughters, without whose forbearance of my long daily absences from the family scene this book would not been at all possible.

Acknowledgement

The quotations attributed to Professor Shenoy were taken from two books, 'Economic Prophecies' and 'Theoretical Vision'. Both are a compilation of essays written by the professor and published by the Center for Civil Society, New Delhi. Other quotations are from the Net, basically the Wikipedia.

I would be failing in my duty if I did not mention my friend S. Ganesan, who through all the months it took to write this book gave me his unstinted support and encouragement.

My grateful thanks to Ms. Yamini Vasudevan for the patience and skill she exhibited in editing this book.

Chapter I

"What should one do, when one does not have the faintest idea of what to do?"

This statement by Ishwar, his colleague, intrigued Paresh Rathore. What should one do? The first thing to do, of course, was to define the problem. But, what about the solution? After thinking hard, he realised that he did not have the faintest idea.

A graduate in electronics engineering, Paresh had worked for a couple of years in industry before going in for an MBA. Like many of his peers, he became a techie. As a manager at a global software company, it was his job to understand complex issues and propose solutions. Paresh's foot danced between the brake and the accelerator as he peered through the rain stained windscreen. The traffic on the Outer Ring road at Marathahalli, Bangalore, was bad. After about 10 minutes of stop-go driving, he felt the need to stretch.

He was tall – about six feet, and wiry, like his father. He was pleasant looking, and his face lit up when he smiled – which was often. He had no dearth of friends and was sought after at parties. He had been a good sportsman at school and college and prided himself on keeping fit.

Now, he needed to concentrate on driving, so he pushed the conundrum out of his mind. The heavy downpour of a few minutes ago had decreased to a few drops. He opened the window and enjoyed the feel of the cold wind in his face and the smell of rain.

Some people were milling about on the street. Those who were working at food stalls started to clean vessels and cook food. A muscular, thick-necked man in a sleeveless vest was stirring something in a big pot. Paresh inhaled a whiff of the pungent biriyani masala; it made him feel hungry. All six feet of him wanted some of that food. Some workmen were slopping cement on a wall, intent on finishing the day's quota of work. Next to them, some men in paint-stained clothes were putting away the tools of their trade. Paresh instinctively looked down at the laptop placed in the passenger seat next to him. That was his tool. He marvelled at the hard physical labour these people put in. His wonder grew when he realised that he had not done an iota of work that day other than to go to meetings. Not a stroke of the pen or keyboard. In conventional terms, he had simply 'wasted' the whole day. However, as a techie at Global Tech, he realised the importance of such meetings. It was at these meetings that the parameters were established, important customer requirements were distilled and broken down into practical work units and timelines set. In the adrenaline-filled world of software engineering, you could not get away from these meetings nor could you fumble at any of them. Mistakes meant curtains for your career, or at least its upward curve. Looked at that way, Paresh had performed well. His job was safe for now, and, in the post-recession world, that was surely a blessing.

Half an hour later, Paresh flopped down wearily on the drawing room sofa. So heavily that some good Kingfisher beer sloshed out of the bottle onto the sofa. That was one more chore to complete. His parents were due to come down from Mumbai in a couple of days. Even if they wouldn't say anything about his light social drinking, he did not like being sloppy. Further, he felt that it was somehow disrespectful to his parents if such traces remained. He was, in that sense, a strange bundle of contradictory emotions and thoughts – modern in outlook, yet clinging to old virtues. If you asked why this was so, he would answer simply that he did not believe in throwing out the baby with the bath water. Sure one must change and accept modernity, yet there were many good things in the old value system that enhanced the quality of life in subtle ways. Why should we throw those away?

Paresh stretched his legs and took another swig of beer. He was still unable to come up with an answer to the riddle posed by Ishwar. He switched on the TV and surfed channels, and let his mind idle. TV was the means through which he caught up with news about the rest of the world and he liked to surf channels unless some programme caught his fancy. Most of the programmes were boring – mother-in-law and daughter-in-law melodramas. He moved on. The next one was a Kannada news channel. After three years in Bangalore, he had learnt a smattering of the language, but could not follow it completely as yet. Anyway, the news was likely to be full of doings and goings on at district level. It could actually be quite depressing. The corruption, the sheer venality, the arrogant brazenness with which politicians cheated the people, while, all the time piously claiming to be serving them, revolted Paresh. Many politicians had even shrugged off the fig leaf of social service that an earlier generation had clung to so tenaciously. The present lot came with such supreme confidence, that their sense of entitlement would have put Roman emperors to shame. They openly pushed, shoved and grabbed with both hands. If they were caught with their hands in the till, it was time for the Party Leader, the Chief Minister or even the Prime Minister to step up to the camera. All that the worthy eminence then needed to do was to mouth a few shibboleths, shush lonely voices raised against blatant corruption, spread innuendo against opponents and fling counter accusations, and then that would be it. It would be back to business as usual, with a jaunty 'theek hai'. A cold anger gripped him every time a corruption racket was exposed. Taxes were cut from his salary by his employer and deposited in the government account. He always felt outraged that this was the money the politicos gorged on every time they got their hands dirty. Indeed, it was as though there was never going to be a time when their hands would be clean. The worst offender in this respect was Nirmal Padamji and his Common Cause Party.

In the next channel, a pretty young lady was shouting, quite breathlessly, at the top of her voice. "This is incredible! There are so many thousands gathered here spontaneously. There is no apparent organisation other than the man himself. Yet the crowds are orderly and well behaved. The crowds surged after SMSes were sent asking them to be present at the Ram Lila maidan."

Paresh sat up. Anything to do with technology and connectivity interested him. He paused to study the scene. It was indeed chaotic, with thousands of people milling about, and from the few grab shots shown, more were streaming in.

The camera moved to a close up of a simple stage set up at one end of the extensive grounds. An old man in a Gandhi cap sat there. The excitement of the crowds seemed wasted on him. It was not that he did not show any emotion, just that there was a sense of calmness on his face. He looked at the crowds serenely, even as several people came to confer with him on the dais. Paresh was hard put to understand what was going on.

"Atmaji has pulled off a minor miracle," the young journalist could hardly contain her excitement. "The mood here is electric and the one thing I want to emphasise is that there is none of the organised crowd control one associates with political parties."

Paresh found it hard to decide whether to continue listening to the journalist, or to read the ticker. He decided on the latter as the young lady seemed to be totally sold out on the size and instantaneous nature of the crowd.

'Atmaji on a fast unto death', the ticker said. He was demanding a Lokpal act. Paresh had not heard of Atmaji, but from the way the reporter was going on and on about him, he seemed to be somebody important, though in a different sort of way. Tata, Birla, Ambani, Narayana Murthy and Premji were names Paresh was familiar with. With a little effort, he could place Indira Gandhi, Vajpayee, Narasimha Rao, Sonia Gandhi or even Narendra Modi. The one politician he liked was Ajit Kumar, the former captain of the Indian hockey team.

But Atmaji was a stretch too far. Surely, Atmaji was not a politician. From what Paresh could make out, he seemed to be some sort of a cross between a social worker and a professional agitator. However, at the moment, Paresh was intrigued not by who Atmaji was, but by what he was saying.

"The country has reached an impossible situation. Prices are going up, but corruption is going up more faster. The money from corruption is going into the pockets of politicians and then into bank accounts in foreign countries. This is the worst stealing of national wealth the country has seen so far. To stop this we need a strong and independent Lokpal. A Lokpal, that can inquire into corruption cases and bring the guilty to book. Everybody from politicians to bureaucrats, police and unfortunately some black sheep in the judicial fraternity are cooperating in this loot. This connection must be broken. Personally, I have nothing to gain. I do not look for any political post or gain from this. As you all may be aware, I have dedicated my life to improve the daily lives of people in villages, using the methods pioneered by Gandhiji and Vinobhaji." At this point Paresh shook his head vigorously. Indeed, he did not know this. This guy looked interesting. He must look him up on the Net.

The camera moved back to the reporter allowing Paresh to get his first good look at her. Thick black hair, parted on the left, framed a broad forehead. What really attracted him was her honey coloured eyes. They looked friendly enough though he had a suspicion that they would turn very cold if anybody tried to get fresh with her.

"There is a huge surge in favour of Atmaji," the reporter was saying. In the background, Paresh could see a sea of people. "This is something that the central government can ignore only at its own peril. From Ram Lila grounds, New Delhi, this is Divya Rao reporting."

Her smile made her look younger than her age, which Paresh thought would be in the mid-20s. Her voice was seductively husky. Her reporting was crisp, showing her grasp and intelligence. Paresh was entranced.

He sat there, staring fixedly at the screen for a few minutes more. The newscast had moved on to other topics. Sure that neither Atmaji nor Divya were likely to return, Paresh switched channels rapidly, hoping to catch another glimpse of them. It was then that he realised that even as Atmaji would fill channel after channel, Divya would not be on any of them. Disappointed with his own stupidity, he resolved to look her up in the social media.

Paresh finished his beer and opened his laptop. He looked up Atmaji first, to learn about his movement. It was a civil society movement – mainly middle-class people like himself were spearheading it. From what he could cull from the sea of material available, it was becoming explosively popular. He felt liberated when he learnt that there were hundreds of thousands like him, who were fed up with the existing cesspool of corruption, lies, and deception and wanted a clean polity. A polity led by ordinary people, and not by the privileged, decadent elite, redolent of Lutyens Delhi. In fact, the leaders of the movement were now beginning to call it a Second Independence movement. Paresh felt lightheaded. Nothing political had excited him so much before.

He saw that the movement had called on every Indian to participate. It dawned on him that there was a big world outside, a world that was alive and kicking and trying to make itself heard – and against all odds. A world consisting of people just like him; people who had previously never bothered about public causes. He felt bad that he had been selfishly absorbed in his own work, in his own world all this time. He now felt the same reverence towards the movement that he associated with a temple or his daily meditation practise. He made a snap decision – he went to the movement's website and registered. Maybe he was late in joining, but he would make up for it through hard work and vigour. He would offer his information technology skills and make as big an impact as possible.

He was a man who enjoyed his dessert; he liked to savour good things leisurely. He decided to learn more about Divya as well. He hesitated, finger poised over the touchpad. He was not sure that this was the ideal time to do so. His finger brushed the hard plastic of the keyboard. After a couple of minutes, he resolved that it could wait for another day. He finished his beer and reached for a slice of cheese chicken pizza – his dinner for the day.

Having finished his dinner and having cleaned up, he was still full of restless energy. He wanted to know and do more for the anti-corruption movement. However much he sought to suppress it, he was unable to keep down a subliminal desire to learn more about Divya. What should he do? The question reminded him of the riddle his friend had posed. What should he do now that he was totally confused? How to break the impasse? He still did not have an answer to the riddle his friend had posed, but he was not the kind to sit and let events overtake him. He decided to take a step; even a small one as this would break the status quo. He opened his computer again and went to his Facebook page, typed in her name and searched. Soon enough, he found her. She had done an M.A in English, and a course in electronic media. He hesitated again before taking the plunge. He sent her a friend request.

Chapter II

It was nearly two years now since joining IndiaNow TV, though, to Divya, it seemed just like yesterday. She chafed under the tight control of her supervisors, but she was honest enough to admit that she had learnt a lot about the art of reporting in that time. She had learnt to stick to the story on hand, show both sides of issues, and keep personal views and emotions out of the reporting.

When the editor had told her to report on the event at Ram Lila, she had been working on background profiling of political leaders across parties. She had managed to link leaders' statements and their actions, pointing to a certain disconnect between the two. Her editor had urged her to dig deeper to put together enough material for a half-hour programme. She was very excited about this her first independent feature. When she left for Ramlila, she had figured on coverage of just a couple of hours.

Nevertheless, a raw excitement gripped her after witnessing the surge of crowds and the sense of hope and optimism that hung over the grounds, like the fragrant smoke from a thousand incense sticks. Speaker after speaker made inspired speeches, clearly from the heart, and managing, repeatedly, to connect to the crowd. The overarching theme was corruption, and their simple but evocative solution of an all-powerful Lokpal that would protect the interests of the common people from the predations of the political class. More than the speeches, it was the magnificent way in which Delhi's masses – rich, poor and middle classes – had responded to Atmaji's call that excited her. Her nose for a good story told her that this would snowball into something very big. It would not be too much to say that the nation as a whole stood on the cusp of a change, and she had said so on screen.

It was almost eight when she got back home. She skipped to her bedroom after a quick 'hello' to her mother. She got rid of her full-sleeve top and the long stole that she had wrapped around her neck. She considered these essential items in a female journalist's wardrobe. She was of average height and well rounded and a shade of brown that made North Indians mistake her for one of them, while South Indians held that she was definitely one of theirs. But there could be no mistaking the sparkle in her large eyes and the fullness of her figure; she was beautiful.

Her mother, thoughtful as ever, had already switched on the geyser. Divya stepped under the shower, letting the warm water massage away the pains and aches of a long and tiring day. She dried herself with a soft turkey towel and put on a kaftan. She brushed her long raven tresses, with a few decidedly casual flicks, before descending for dinner. She felt very hungry.

"What's there?" she asked loudly even before hitting the last step of the stairway.

"Chappatis, alu sabji,palak, raita and curd," her mother called from the dining room. Divya's face fell. "And, of course, there is mutton samosa from Rajiv's." Divya perked up.

"Give me the samosa first." She grabbed it from her mother's hand.

"Wait, wait," Mrs. Rao spluttered ineffectually. Divya was already gorging on the samosa.

"If you eat that first, you hardly eat anything else, especially nourishing vegetables and palak."

"Mother!" Divya almost shrieked. "I am not 10 years old. I am 25 now, if you can manage to remember it."

Her mother nodded. "That's the point I wish to make. I am glad you acknowledge that you are 25. You should know your responsibilities by now. Look at the careless way in which you have made up your hair. It is so pretty; still, you do not seem to realise that many people will choose you just for that."

"Don't," Divya hissed, "talk to me about marriage again. I will go away and not eat my dinner." This was a threat that worked, always.

"No, no, not at all." Sushila Rao shook her head vigorously, making soothing noises. "All I am saying is that all this running around...I am sure Ranjit, Ajay, Meenakshi and your friends are good boys and girls. But do you have to spend night after night in their homes?"

"I don't spend nights out with Ranjit or Ajay," Divya could barely suppress her anger.

"I don't say you do, but what about Meenakshi or Lavanya? I am not against partying. God knows this is the phase of life when you can indulge. But you should keep some limits."

"Are you scared about my eligibility for marriage?" Divya said in an unmistakably menacing tone.

"What I mean is that you should take better care of your health."

"Look Ma," Divya said, stuffing the last piece of chappati in her mouth. Sushila waited patiently for Divya to finish chewing.

"I like the good life and I am a journalist by choice. People can talk – they do anyway even if you are goody-goody, which I am not. I do what I think is right, and you cannot say that as occasion demands I don't mind being guided by you or Pa. Please understand I want to make a mark in journalism. This demands that I meet people and socialise and keep on top of news. News that you see in a newspaper or on TV is the final product. Behind it lie hundreds of parties, as any good journalist will attest to. Beyond that, I leave it to fate. Anyhow, I believe God helps those who help themselves. So don't worry about me. I know how to take care of myself and I will settle down, but in my own good time." With that firm statement, in the same fashion that a first-rate power gives a demarche to a third rate power, she swept out of the room.

Divya seethed with indignation. Was marriage the only legitimate objective for a young woman? Was that all her mother could think of? This made her so angry that her head started to throb. She flung herself on the bed and pulled a pillow over her face. Her breathing was forced and uneven. To divert her thoughts, she dreamt of a holiday in Thailand with a suitable hero-like guy. After a few minutes, she began to feel better. Her breathing became more regular and she fell asleep, but without checking her mail and Facebook page.

Nirmal Padamji was the pampered scion of one the political dynasties that had ruled India for a long time. He was a very fair, handsome man. Though he needed heels to reach six feet, he took care to keep very fit, even muscular. He carried his birth and position in life easily, though in his dark eyes was a hint of menace that told anybody who was bold enough to look into them that they dare not mess with him. His view on life was simple, as he often told his intimate friends – he was born to rule and rule he would, though the means he adopted to that end would change as circumstances demanded. Other than that, he refused to discuss any philosophy.

He awoke with a start. He felt the comforting warmth of Denise, who was still asleep beside him. It was a chilly spring morning in London and he drew the sheets tightly around him. He closed his eyes hoping for more sleep, but found it difficult. He turned around to look at the clock. It was 7.30a.m.; it would be 12 o'clock in India. He had to get up. Yet, he was loathe to leave his bed and the warmth of Denise's nude body. He threw the covers back violently with a loud oath. The noise and the sudden deprivation of the comforting sheets awoke Denise.

"What is it?" Her voice was still sleepy and she tried to reach the sheets to pull back on.

Nirmal merely grunted, not bothering to reply. Denise might belong to a respectable British family, but for Nirmal she was something he did at night and occasionally by day.

Her questions did not merit an answer unless it addressed some of the things he wanted.

"You," he whispered, kissing her cheek softly.

Denise pushed him away.

"Now?" She was hardly ready for another time.

"Yes." Nirmal's voice was firm. Her warmth aroused him. He cupped the softness of her breast in his palm, gently tightening his hold.

"No, not now."

He squeezed her breast mercilessly.

"Oww! That hurt!" she gasped.

He didn't waste any more time. He turned and pinned her on the bed with a strong muscular thigh. She resisted, or tried to. He was too strong for her and the squeeze had hurt. She gave in.

He mounted her, clasping her palms and pushing her hands aside at right angles to her shoulder so that she lay sprawled. He managed to find her inner recess by himself. Comfortably settled, he sought her mouth and kissed her hard. All too soon, he sighed heavily and she felt his slimy wetness. He rolled off.

"You are a peach, Denise." His voice was lovingly soft. Denise was not deceived. She knew he had her where he wanted her, and he could have her whenever he wanted. She turned round with a sigh, seeking cold comfort in the now disarranged sheets.

He had hardly finished his toilet routine when the phone rang.

It was Patel, his trusted assistant. Atmaji had invited Ajit to address the crowds at Ramlila. There was a desperate urgency to Patel's tone, as if he expected Padamji to transpose himself back to Delhi by magic. Nirmal did not have to be told the consequences, though this is exactly what Patel did, and in excruciating detail. Patel was a valuable assistant and Nirmal was not averse to giving him some rope, from time to time. He sighed; he would show his annoyance at this disturbance later.

"That's alright. So what if Ajit talks? We will tell the world that that's all he can do. A rabble-rouser can hardly be an epitome of governance, and the ability to govern is what we will focus on. Anyway, don't say anything yet, and tell Narain too. Nothing blatant; just keep your reactions soft, as in, it is everybody's right to speak and so forth."

Divya, on the other hand, could hardly contain herself. The unexpected news that Ajit Kumar would be speaking had galvanised the crowds. Atmaji had been strict in not allowing any politicos to take the stage and usurp credit for the extraordinary upsurge that Ram Lila maidan had witnessed. Divya was excited that Ajit had been invited, as this would put him squarely against Padamji. How would Padamji react to this?

Since Ajit was slated to address the gathering only at noon, Divya found herself with time on her hands after the first coverage for the day was over. She got down to checking her mail and Facebook from her Blackberry. She saw that she had a friend request from somebody called Paresh. She received these requests regularly. She clicked the 'Yes' button and thought no more of it. She was sure that, some day, some of her many Facebook 'friends' would come in useful. Just when, where, how, or why, she did not know.

"How come Ajit is allowed to speak, while all other politicos are banned?" Divya asked Preeti, a senior colleague.

"Atmaji has allowed him to talk," Preeti said, "as he handled a social movement that he keeps separate from his political activities. In his heyday as India's hockey centre forward, he acted in several commercials – virtually the only hockey player to do so. The money he made from this was shared with his teammates. Using these film contacts, he set up a benevolent fund to help all the people concerned with the game, like grounds men and umpires, making the first contribution himself.

"He is obsessed with the concept of teamwork. He sincerely feels that Indians in general are poor team players. He encouraged the youth in slums and other disadvantaged sections of the populace to play games. Any game, be it cricket, hockey, football, basketball or volleyball; the only criterion was that it should be a team game.

"This proved to be a popular initiative. As a National Volunteer, he made full use of that network for this purpose. His efforts caught the imagination of the people, especially the under-privileged, who felt that they had a strong champion for their cause. Moreover, he was a champion who would not be swayed by caste or other sectarian influences, a champion who had put India first. Hence, Atmaji had consented that Ajit could address the crowds at Ram Lila."

"Padamji, the President of the Common Cause Party, is not invited. Won't this pose a problem to Atmaji's Movement? Won't it be seen as partisan?"asked Divya,by now a staunch supporter of Atmaji. She was afraid that the movement would get embroiled in petty politics.

"Well, Padamji is a traditional politician and dynast to boot. Atmaji, in fact, first offered to cooperate with the CCP in finding a solution."

"What happened?"

"They simply ignored him. You must not forget that the entire anti-corruption movement is aimed against the unprecedented levels of corruption the present CCP government is accused of. It is common knowledge that both Padamji and the CCP are utterly corrupt, even if this can't be proved in a court of law. Their aim is to keep the dynasty safe and keep on ruling the country."

Ajit did not disappoint. He took care to keep his political affiliations out of the picture. He emphasised the need for civil society to act to curb corruption and warmly praised Atmaji's leadership. The only jarring note that he struck was that, alone among the speakers, he said that appointing a Lokpal alone would not contain corruption. The entire governmental machinery, which was organised to extract 'rents', had to be completely overhauled and downsized, to curb corruption. In the surcharged atmosphere, Divya was not sure if this different approach to preventing corruption received the attention that it merited.

After a few days the central government relented and started negotiations with Atmaji's team. One of Atmaji's key aide, Ranjan Das, was nominated as the point man for the talks. After some back and forth, Ranjan obtained an agreement from the government that they would introduce a Lokpal bill. Since time was short, it would be introduced in the winter session of the parliament rather than immediately as demanded by Atmaji. Sensing victory, Atmaji agreed.

Ajit Kumar, however, voiced reservations and issued a statement that the government could not be trusted and that they would make use of every opportunity to delay the bill. Ranjan surprised everyone by saying that he had faith in the government. Ajit could very well introduce a private member's bill, if he was not satisfied. For good measure, Ranjan also claimed that the bill should not be soiled by someone whose views were tainted by the Right. The innuendo was unmistakable – Ranjan had hit the target. The liberal newspapers and their reporters and columnists echoed this line and the movement lost its momentum.

Chapter III

Paresh stretched comfortably in his bed and let his mind wander over the events of the previous few days. The size of the crowds at the Ramlila grounds was an eye opener. It provoked his dormant political instincts. He wanted to get involved, but just did not know how. There, he told himself, was that question again. What to do when you do not know what to do? It was amazing how this question kept cropping up in his life, ever since Ishwar had first posed it.

Several theories were doing the rounds in Delhi regarding Ranjan's volte-face. One was that some industrialists had bribed him, as their business interests would be affected. Another was that Ranjan was only after publicity. He would soon start another agitation on another matter and try to grab eyeballs on national TV.

Paresh was not convinced that any of them was really the truth. None of them seemed to make sense. Ranjan was already a hero, and could only have grown bigger if the agitation had continued. Admittedly, the agitation had begun to lose steam, particularly when the government had held firm. The strongest glue holding agitators together in any cause is the hope that their adversary would give in totally to their demands. Even if not fully, to at least to engage with them to arrive at a consensus. In the present case, neither had happened. The government remained a mute spectator to the big crowds, providing only minimal police protection. Government spokespersons too offered only bland statements, such as, "We respect Atmaji and his movement". The one that took the cake for Paresh was, "We support Atmaji on his courageous crusade against corruption and his efforts for a Lokpal". This position conveniently sidestepped the fact that the movement was in fact aimed at the mega scams by the incumbent government, and, if an ombudsman or Lokpal had to be appointed, it was the responsibility of the government to bring and pass a Lokpal Act in Parliament.

Clearly, the government had thought through all this. Paresh sensed that the brain behind the government's strategy was Padamji. Under a genial and cherubic exterior, Paresh realised, was a wily and scheming mind, a powerful intellect that could pull the wool over one's eyes just as easily as it could cause a knife to be sunk into one's back. On the political stage, there were few to rival his Machiavellian brain.

In another direction, his thoughts were drawn repeatedly to Divya, though he had seen her just a couple of times on TV. The urge to communicate with her kept on bubbling up inside him, like lava from a seething volcano. She was in Delhi and he in Bangalore, she was a TV journalist and he was a software engineer. There was little or no chance of their meeting. In fact it would be only pure chance, if they ever met. He could not understand this growing fixation. Though he told himself several times that "this is just silly", he was unable to shake off the feeling. Divya had this tendency to pop up in his mind whenever he was in front of a electronic screen, which was pretty much the whole day.

After a couple of days, Paresh decided that he had had enough. He would try to establish contact with her. If it worked, well and good; if it did not, then maybe he could, in good conscience, put an end to the issue. The question once again was what to do, even though he had not the faintest idea what that was. He could take a first small step in his attempt to remedy the situation. He found a good idea to open the conversation.

He would ask Divya about the Ranjan angle. What if Padamji had got to Ranjan? Paresh, marshalling the evidence, saw that this was a distinct possibility. Upto a certain day, Ranjan had been bashing Padamji and the CCP; then, suddenly, he had started questioning the 'right wing' Bharatiya Ganatantra Party or BGP. Had he stopped with that, it would have been entirely unremarkable. What angered Paresh and set him thinking even more seriously was that the fact that Ranjan had targeted Ajit personally. This had surprised many others too. Indeed, several newspapers had devoted a good many column inches to the issue.

Paresh would use this idea to open a conversation with Divya. He decided that he would mail her in the evening and call her the next day. This would give her the time to read his mail and respond. No thought that she might not be willing to discuss such sensitive matters with a perfect stranger ever crossed his mind.

He decided to call her from a public booth. That way he would remain anonymous, and Divya, if she was questioned, could always say that it was yet another call she received in her line of duty as a journalist. Of course, for the mainstream media, Padamji, his family in particular, and the CCP in general, were the very embodiment of liberal virtues. Paresh was not prepared to underestimate the lengths to which Padamji and the CCP would go to silence critics.

Paresh dialled Divya's number, which was listed on Facebook. To Paresh's intense annoyance, the phone went on ringing till it stopped. Not one to be deterred by such setbacks, Paresh redialled –without success. He took a deep breath and waited for a minute. He decided to change tactics and call her from his mobile. That way, she would see his number and he could speak to her when she called back. "Third time lucky," he told himself without much conviction and drew another deep breath before dialling. The phone rang several times before a mature and feminine voice hesitantly answered. "Hello."

Paresh wondered why she was so unsure, in answering a simple phone call. However, he decided to match Divya and said "Hello" in a low voice. It was too soft, so he quickly corrected it with a louder, more masculine "Hello".

The voice on the other side returned the 'Hello' in a stronger voice, but it did not sound like the voice of a cute 20-something. Had he made a mistake in the number? Paresh wiped his brow.

"Divya?" The hesitancy in his voice was genuine.

"Mrs. Rao," said the voice on the other end stiffly.

Panic now firmly gripped Paresh. Was Divya married? He was so surprised that he was at a loss for words.

"Who is it?" Mrs. Rao asked in an authoritative voice. Paresh was still unable to make any reply.

"I am Divya's mother. Who are you and what do you want?" This was in a coaxing tone.

Relieved, Paresh cleared his throat noisily to cover his confusion. He struck his forehead lightly at his own stupidity.

"I want to talk to her." How could he tell Mrs. Rao, that he had met Divya only on Facebook and wanted to talk to her about serious political matters as a ruse to developing a conversation?

"She has a headache and is resting. Shall I ask her to call you later?"

"Yes...yes, would be most obliged if you could do that." By now, he was in no condition to talk to Divya or anybody else.

"Your name?"

"Paresh." He disconnected gratefully.

Later that day, he had recovered sufficiently to speak with his usual self-confidence when Divya called.

"Hello, my Mother told me that you wished to speak to me."

"Oh yes, good evening. How are you?"

"I am fine and I hope you are good."

Paresh cleared his throat.

"I am Paresh..."

"I know, Mom told me."

"I...ah would like to talk to you about..." What had seemed a brilliant idea just that morning now appeared weak and contrived. Lacking alternatives, he decided to go on.

"You know this Atmaji's movement...Gee, you covered that really well."

"Thanks. What about Atmaji?"

"What I was about to say was that...Why did it collapse?"

Divya didn't hesitate. "The answer is obvious. They got what they wanted."

Paresh became strong again.

"But that is the question I want to ask. Did they get all that they wanted? They just have a vague assurance from the government about a new law, which may not contain the clauses they want to put in." Paresh went on not daring to stop for a breath. "Why did Ranjan suddenly agree with the government and almost from the same time start attacking Ajit?"

"I don't know."

Paresh felt his enthusiasm waning. "Maybe those two have a deal?"

"Which two?"

"Padamji and Ranjan."

"Not likely, even if that were so it is no big thing. All these things are common in politics."

Paresh swooped on this point like a bird of prey. "That is exactly my point." He tried hard to keep the excitement out of his voice. "Ranjan is no different from and no better than any of the other politicians, though he claims to be pure and above it all."

Paresh heard something that sounded suspiciously like a yawn. "Here in Delhi, everybody knows that. Yet, no one can deny that he has indeed brought in a whiff of fresh air to the political scene. And that is his selling point. Nice talking to you Mr. Paresh but I have to go."

"Can you ask somebody if my theory is correct?"

"Uh...oh...very well. I will ask some of my colleagues. You have got a good point and, from my experience, I can say that you are right. What do you do Mr. Paresh?"

"I am a software engineer, a senior Consultant with Global Tech" Paresh was justly proud of his profession.

"Ah, that accounts for your sharpness, Mr. Paresh. Goodbye and have a nice day."

Paresh clutched the now silent phone to his ear, unwilling to believe that Divya had really cut the line. Reluctantly he put his mobile back in his pocket. He did not know if he had made the desired impact. All he had to console himself with was that now she had his number and knew his name. But was that enough to keep him in her memory?

Divya could not help laughing as she switched off. This was the most bizarre approach she had been subjected to in her young life. But she could see his point of view too. If you wanted to open a conversation with a TV journalist like herself, you could hardly go wrong if the subject was politics.

Chapter IV

"Good evening. This is Primetime News at eight from India Global TV. I am Tony Rai. Next week, the Bharatiya Ganatantra Party General Council meets to elect a new President. Ajit Kumar will be stepping down after the two terms permitted by the BGP's constitution."

"Devender Anand is widely expected to be elected the next President. Our sources say that the deal is all tied up, and he will be chosen by consensus. For an in-depth view on this story, let's go across to Shantanu Ghosh."

For Paresh, this was a surprise. He had assumed that Ajit would continue to be President. He was unaware of the party's constitutional niceties. He wondered if there was anyone else capable enough to replace him.

"Shantanu, how do you see the two terms of Ajit's President-ship, and what is in store for the party in the future?"

"To give credit where it is due, Ajit completely overhauled the party, right from the basic structures to the top policy making and planning bodies. He focussed on professionalising the party organisation. For example, today, the BGP has a post for a media secretary, whose main job is to analyse the various reports about the party in the media and to coach its spokespersons."

"Do you reckon that Padamji and CCP should also develop something similar?"

"I don't think it is my place to advise the CCP, but, yes, I think something on the lines of a media secretary would certainly be helpful, particularly in this era of information overload. Don't forget that Ajit personally makes brilliant use of the social media as well."

"How do you see the General Council meeting tomorrow? Will the meeting run according to script or will there be any fireworks? Our sources tell us that there is growing tension between Ajit and Lalwani, the senior leader."

"Yes, that is right. Lalwani, who was initially supportive of Ajit's efforts to spruce up the party, is now taking a different stance. This may be caused by Ajit's growing popularity, not only among the party cadre, but also amongst the general public."

"What do you think Lalwani will do?"

"I don't know. Lalwani is an experienced player, and knows how to play this game well. Devender enjoys Lalwani's support and everyone knows that Lalwani is still not reconciled to BGP's defeat in the last general elections. If you recall, the party had fully backed him and yet it came up with one of its lowest vote shares and seat tallies. I think he still harbours ambitions of becoming PM."

"Do you think that ambition would materialise, given that Ajit is thought to be equally if not more popular?"

"I don't think you can compare the two of them like that. Lalwani is a veteran of many political battles, a founding father of the party, and receives immense respect from party workers. Ajit is a role model for many people, and not just for his hockey skills. Remember, those ads he did in the 1980s; and donating the major part to players, grounds men and needy people connected with game. Indeed he even financed a part of the playing kit for the national team from these earnings. He is popular for this Robin Hood nature of his. This is the stuff that legends are made of. You may say that Ajit has carefully built up this do-gooder image. Nevertheless, at some time in the past he actually did these good things and his only aim was to see the team win. This certainly has a special resonance with the people, be it the middle-class or the poor. At the same time, Ajit did very well as Minister of Education the last time the BGP was in power. And, ever since, he has carefully nursed the youth constituency. Don't forget that, in the coming elections, first-time voters are expected to be about 20% of the electorate. I think that Ajit does have his own political game plan. I would not underestimate him at all."

"What of Padamji, who has also been courting the same constituency?"

"That is a different story altogether, isn't it?"

"Yes! I think we can leave that for another day. Thanks very much." The shot ended with Rai grinning like a Cheshire cat.

Paresh, disgusted at Rai's partisan approach, handed the remote to his bored-looking mother and retreated to his bedroom. His view of Ajit was now a bit clearer. He felt that, compared to the rest of the crowd, Ajit was better. If

Ajit didn't politicise issues, play politics, dirtily if necessary, he would not be able survive the labyrinthine world of Indian politics. If Ajit was completely straightforward, how different would he be from Paresh and millions of others in the great Indian middle-class? Paresh swallowed with a little difficulty. Ajit had to play hardball to survive and overcome his foes. Paresh's only consolation was that Ajit's thinking, ideology and actions were good and that his heart was in the right place.

Chapter V

"I thank the Finance Minister for explaining why some industries need help and how he has afforded them that help. These industries, particularly the auto industry, deserves help as it generates a lot of employment. I commend him for his brave attempt to set right the market conditions so that these industries can flourish and enrich India."

Ajit could not but help wonder how much money had changed hands to bring about this happy conclusion.

"In a democracy..." Ajit really liked the way Padamji said the 'd-word' in such a caressing tone. "In a democracy, we must forever be vigilant against the majority tyrannising the minority. This is what our government believes in and practises in its day to day working." Padamji sat down beaming, even as the CCP benches exploded with applause.

"I am sure my friend Shri Padamji means well." A look of annoyance crossed Padamji's handsome face before he put on his mask of cultivated geniality. The slip, however, did not escape Ajit. Padamji obviously did not like being called 'my friend' by Ajit. The high fans in the Lok Sabha seemed incapable of relieving the hot confrontational atmosphere.

"However, I am unable to agree with him when he says that the current measures would improve the national economy. In fact, it is a classic example of asymmetric democracy.

"Mancur Olson, in his book *The Logic of Collective Action*, says that individuals in a group have incentives to take a free ride on the work of others in the group. For example, it would be easy for say three car manufacturers to band together and lobby the government to allow them to increase prices, and they will get to share the gains in equal proportion. Naturally this would affect the interests of the much larger group of car consumers. However most consumers would be content to allow a few to fight against the price rises, while they themselves remain quiet; mainly because the benefit from price reduction for millions of individual car owners would be small. The fight by a few is unlikely to be successful. Thus narrow interest lobbies win out.

"Mind you, higher tariffs make cars more expensive and keep them eternally out of reach of the masses. Yet, according to Shri Padamji's logic, the increase in prices, due to increased tariffs, would be in the interests of the car-consuming public. We have a situation where the car companies are actively lobbying the government, while the larger car-buying public is silent.

"The cost of organising smaller groups are significantly lower and the benefits to members are very much higher than the larger groups. Hence the case for the capability of a minority to oppress the majority is equally strong. Let me make it clear that a minority does not refer only to religious, linguistic or caste minorities. Even more important than all these, are those who dare to think differently. Those heroes who prefer to be right even if they are in a minority of one. Protection of minorities should really mean the protection of these stalwart souls."

Possessed with an ego the size of Mount Everest, Padamji stood up, his face growing redder by the second. "Sir, in many cases, coalitions of poor people have banded together and obtained results. I think my friend is being unnecessarily pessimistic. Let me remind him about how, earlier, our government passed an act in response to an agitation by displaced persons. That act ensures that all displaced persons have a right to livelihood if their lands are taken over for a factory, dam, airport or any other economic activity. The lobbying was done by hundreds of people including adivasis and other depressed sections of society under my leadership.

"Again, on retrospective taxes, Mr. Ajit Kumar is wrong. Does he believe that, for example the taxes collected over a period of ten years should be returned, merely because of a court order? Would he then sit quietly, impotently, while rich men reclaim paid taxes? I say that we must have retrospective taxes when the exchequer is likely to lose. Judiciary also should be committed to the welfare of the nation. Our government stands for the poor. We must collect taxes so that the government can do good to the poor. I go further and say that we must enact retrospective taxes if some businessmen resort to tax avoidance and seek to escape taxes by conducting transactions in third countries. All taxes are to the good of the public at large."

"In a democracy," Ajit replied, deliberately echoing Padamji, "there are three branches of government.

Government or the State, is a creature of Man, made up by citizens. It runs on the basis of an agreement between citizens to deal fairly with each other. That agreement in political terms is called the 'Constitution'. This constitution provides for three branches of public governance. The Legislature, with the authority to make law and to mandate taxes– this also embodies the principle that there should be no taxation without representation. The Executive exercises the powers delegated to it by the laws passed by the Legislature in accordance with the Constitution. The Judiciary interprets the laws, so that the Executive and Legislature branches of the government function in the manner intended in the Constitution.

"The checks and balances inherent in this system are to ensure that no branch of government oversteps its authority and damages individual citizens. This is called the Rule of Law, where everybody has to abide by the laws of the land. Disputes are settled by recourse to cases filed in courts and people are held innocent till proved guilty.

"If a court has interpreted a law in a particular manner that does not suit the Executive and further, if resort is made to the Legislature to amend the law, then where is the need for a Judiciary at all? The other two branches can very well place any interpretation they think is right on the laws and carry on. What Mr. Padamji suggests smacks of totalitarianism, where one group, makes the law, enforces it, and also interprets it. It does not brook a point of view that is contrary to the all-powerful Executive, even if that opinion is within the bounds of law.

"This is further compounded when a retrospective law is made, that too for collecting a tax. Look at it this way. A person at that historical point of time has followed the law as it stood then. The government takes him or her to court and the court delivers a verdict in the individual's favour. The government then shifts the goalposts, so to speak, and amends the act retrospectively. Thus, while the reality is that the individual has followed the law, as upheld by the court, the Executive arrogates to itself the power to amend the law, only to satisfy its gargantuan appetite for tax and ego. The person who was originally not guilty of violating the law is now cast on the wrong side of the law. If for every adverse court order the Executive because of its control over the Legislature amends laws retrospectively or otherwise, then why at all have a court procedure? Can this be called justice? In fact it violates all canons of natural justice. Retrospective taxes are bad in law and repugnant to civilised human society. It will destroy the trust between government and the people.

"Going by Shri Padamji's logic, if collecting taxes is wholly good for the public, why doesn't he try to collect the entire income of the populace as tax? If the entire income is confiscated, and the name given for such confiscation is 'tax', then that 100% tax would entirely benefit society at large?

"The reality is that tax is a confiscation of income, mandated by law, for certain clearly understood 'public' purposes, like maintenance of law and order, basic infrastructure including basic education, external defence and so on. When the State starts to encroach on the other areas, normally the prerogative of the citizens at large, it commits the sin of trampling on their rights.

"The theory of the 'Supremacy of Parliament' has worked havoc with the system of checks and balances. This has resulted in a dysfunctional system. The time has come to set right these anomalies and to return the government system to the pristine purity envisaged by the Fathers of the Constitution, which, may I remind you, included Dr. Ambedkar."

Padamji who had risen to rebut Ajit, sat down abruptly his supercilious smile wiped from his face, when Ajit invoked Dr. Ambedkar. He cast a malevolent look at Ajit before stomping off, growling, "We will test all these nonsense theories at the hustings."

Ajit looked around him, savouring his triumph. He looked around at his colleagues, eagerly seeking acknowledgement of his victory. He was surprised at the look of hostility from several members, including senior leader Lalwani.

Chapter VI

'Ajit sizzled', Divya wrote. 'Yeah, way to go', Paresh replied. They were chatting online.

'I hope the BGP will get its act together now. CCP is a party that must be decimated. Your five cents?'

'Sure', Divya responded. 'BGP is certainly better, but take Ajit Kumar out and the two look ominously similar. BGP has its own Lutyens group, which behaves much like Padamji and the CCP. There is also a tussle in the party about whether to name, and if so, who to name as the PM candidate. Wish Ranjan does something. If he starts a party he can really start on a clean slate. A new broom sweeps clean.'

Paresh was taken aback. He was under the impression that Divya was in Ajit's camp, heart and soul. Her reply seemed to indicate otherwise. Paresh felt bad; it had not occurred to him that Divya could differ from him on any matter.

He knew something about Ajit, but Ranjan was a closed book. He would have to research Ranjan on the Internet. He was more of a NGO activist, with hardly any experience in government. Paresh's gut feeling was that whatever Ranjan's merits, and however genuine they maybe, the coming election was really about Ajit. The BGP leader had a good track record while in government. He had taken the trouble to educate himself properly and previously had worked for the Hong Kong Monetary Authority. All in all, he was an able administrator and a safe hand.

'We will know soon as both CCP and the BGP are to hold their National Council meetings to decide political strategy.' Divya signed off.

Narain, one of the 10 Vice-Presidents of the CCP was droning on and on. Padamji wished he would stop. He smothered a yawn and pretended to focus on what Narain was saying. Personally, Padamji thought that this effort merited an Oscar. At last, Narain, rotund and perspiring, despite the AC temperature set at 21degrees, sat down and reached for the glass of water placed before him. Padamji clapped loudly, lazing in his seat. This was placed to one side of the vast pinewood horseshoe shaped table; the head of the table was left empty. This was his idea of impressing viewers visually with his 'humility'.

"I know that I speak for all of you, when I say that our dear friend Narain has made the most thorough analysis of the present political situation." Narain looked very gratified. No doubt he would expect a plum cabinet after the CCP yet again won the forthcoming General Elections, Padamji mused. "While I do not wish to sound pessimistic, I must urge all present here and all our party workers to give of their best. The coming election won't be easy, and the one thing I do agree with Mr. Ajit Kumar on is that it could well change the fate of the country. We cannot let the elections change the nation's fate. We cannot afford to lose this election. We must fight with all our might and see that Ajit and the BGP are put in their place." Padamji allowed himself a smile. "Of course, the opposition would damn us, or rather me and my family for being dynastic." Instantly, there was uproar, with everyone loudly shouting their support for Padamji. He waited patiently for the tumult to die down, a saintly expression on his fair face.

"We should see through their game and strive to do our best...for the nation. Naturally, they will raise the many allegations of corruption again and again. As we all know this is only a lie." Heads nodded vigorously around the table. A cynic would have said that they could hardly disagree as they had been the secondary beneficiaries of all these 'allegations'. Padamji was, of course, always the primary beneficiary. Since he did not hold a governmental office, he could never be accused of corruption.

"I propose that we nominate Shri Padamji as our PM candidate," Narain said in a loud voice. There was a chorus of approval around the table. Padamji casually glanced at Patel, while acknowledging the cheers.

Patel cleared his throat delicately. "My dear friends," he looked around at each one of those present, passing over only Padamji. "I am sure that if we win…In fact, we will definitely win, there can be no doubt that our revered leader Shri Padamji might well be elected the Prime Minister. Does anyone here doubt that?" Heads shook hard. Padamji looked appreciatively at Patel, who continued, "Equally, we would be subject to attacks on promoting dynasty if we nominate Shri Padamji as PM candidate? Does anyone disagree? No?

Good." He took a sip of water. "So, I don't think that it would be a good idea to nominate anyone as PM candidate."

Narottam Yadav, the party's Uttar Pradesh chief, had a question. "The BGP is likely to announce its own PM candidate, most likely Ajit. In that case, wouldn't we be at a disadvantage if we do not have a clear candidate for PM?"

"Good question." All eyes turned adoringly towards Padamji, but he seemed content with saying just those two words.

"Not really," Patel continued. "Even without nominating anyone, everyone knows that Shri Padamji is our leader. Thus people will have no doubt at all that he will be –in fact, is –their leader too."

All the members of the National Working Committee clapped hard, with Narain in the lead. "Whatever we do, the BGP, and in particular that Ajit..." A filthy oath audible to all escaped Padamji's mouth. Everyone continued looked at Patel; not a single muscle moved in any of those 30 faces. "As I was saying," Patel continued smoothly, "BGP will damn us for being dynastic if we nominate Shri Padamji, and castigate us for being confused if we didn't. The way to play the game is to keep cool. Let them say what they will. We will stick to our line that BGP wants only power, while our leaders are thinking of labouring for the toiling masses."

"Well said." Padamji put his hands together and was instantly joined by all the others, Patel included. Padamji got up –the signal that the meeting had ended.

Chapter VII

Paresh reserved Saturday mornings for his personal chores and the evenings for fun activities; Sundays were meant for snoozing. This Saturday would be no different. He made coffee without waking his mother and put on his sweatshirt and running shoes. He let himself out of the flat quietly and went for his morning run. The weather was pleasant in Bangalore, as it was on most days – but today, it seemed to be uncommonly good. The morning air was crisp, with just that invigorating bite of a chill in it. Paresh hit his stride right away and loped around the perimeter of the gated community. It was around a kilometre long and he normally did three rounds. Today he decided to do one more. He then went to the gym for a workout before returning home. On the way back, he heard the TV blaring.

"This is big news that can change the dynamics of the Lok Sabha election…"

Paresh tuned out the sound. These guys were always going on and on like this. Maybe they needed to do that, as it was part of their job. He could not be bothered with inanities that were passed off as breaking news. It was not as if Ajit Kumar had made some statement or something like that. Ajit was serious, he worked hard, did his homework and took reasonable positions on issues. Paresh would not mind listening to Ajit, but the others were passé –particularly Padamji. If there was one politician Paresh genuinely hated, it was Padamji. He could hardly stand that thug's arrogance.

As he entered his house, he stopped dead in his tracks. His father was watching IndiaNow TV and Kiran Butt was saying something in that horribly simpering way she had, that Ajit had called for a press conference at 10, and that there could be a split in the BGP.

Tired now in mind, as well as in body, he turned away for making a cup of rejuvenating Nilgiris tea when he saw Divya behind Kiran on the TV screen. He needed no more inducement. He sat down beside his father and hollered to his mother for the tea.

His mind was in a whirl. Like many of his peers, Paresh had been hoping that the BGP would nominate Ajit for PM. This was necessary as Ajit alone looked like he was capable of getting the country out of the rut into which it had fallen. Apparently that had not happened.

Ajit had modern ideas, he was honest, and he had proved his administrative ability in his stint as the nation's education minister. Try as they might, the CCP were unable to undo the good he had done. Not only that, Ajit had fought courageously, quite often alone, against every effort to undo the new educational policy. The policy had become a game-changer for the youth, who could now choose from a wide variety of courses. What Ajit had done was to adopt the successful vocational training system of Germany, while improving the university-based approach of Britain that India had inherited.

He had innovated too, such as with the introduction of three-year 'Professional' degree courses. Upon realising that diploma courses were deemed to be lower down the ladder than degree courses, Ajit had introduced 'Professional' degree courses. These ran the usual three years, but, instead of teaching academic subjects such as physics, mathematics, literature or history alone, Ajit and his advisors had come up with a course that would keep academic subjects as a base while expanding into a wide portfolio of vocational courses as 'electives'. For example, a literature student could do journalism along with the regular subjects; physics student could do either electronic media, photography or computer science. In a first for the bureaucratised moribund Indian education system, these courses were actively 'marketed' to the students. Again, Ajit and his advisors selected the vocational subjects after consultation with business associations. Thus, students who completed these courses could look forward to immediate employment. Businesses were also happy that they could get qualified hands to man a rapidly growing economy. Another dimension to this new system was that students could pursue a wide range of courses in the form of postgraduate diplomas. Ajit's research had shown that there was no antipathy to the word 'postgraduate diploma'. Students could pursue specialisation in chosen fields, or take diplomas in allied subjects to broaden their skill sets. What caught the attention of the press and the nation was his 'Management Extension Service'. This was conceived as akin to the agriculture extension service introduced during the Green Revolution. Ajit reasoned that if largely illiterate farmers could understand and make use of new technology, so too could traders and small-scale businessmen. The scheme involved the use of talent available at the Institutes of Management to advise small businessmen, even hawkers, on how to improve their business models, with advice given on maintaining stocks, sales strategies and obtaining finance. Above all, he realised that these people needed not only finance but also financial advice. Started as a pilot project along with the concerned ministries, Ajit had scaled it up rapidly. Within a period of two years, about 70% of the country had been covered. The balance would take at least another two years to penetrate. Many had praised this model for the quick results it had brought and the boost it had given to economy by increasing the base of the pyramid of growth. From Ajit's point of view, while these were important and laudable objectives, what mattered most was that he had been able to bring some positive change to the lives of the people under the scheme. If they made just another 20% or 30% more money, that would be a huge gain for these people, who lived on the margins of existence.

It was an entirely different matter that Padamji lampooned this as a technocratic scheme that did not benefit the people in the 30% of the territory left out. This was turned into an electoral plank and the press gave it as one of the reasons for the CCP's subsequent triumph in the elections.

A tap on the shoulder brought him out of his reverie. He eagerly reached for the cup of tea his mother was holding. On screen, Kiran Butt was positively drooling when she announced that the BGP had split over the naming of a PM candidate. Ajit had quit the party and would announce his plans shortly. As he sipped, he found that the hot tea did not have its usual 'kick'.

Chapter VIII

"The party's name is Jan Awaaz Party (People's Voice). I have chosen this name after much thought. The problem with the present situation is that the common man or woman's voice is hardly ever heard. Not only that, the channels for communication with the government is mostly clogged. This has led to noise –the noise of the mobs, paid or otherwise, and has diminished the common people's voice. The ability of the ordinary man or woman to express his/her thoughts without fear is getting lower all the time.

"JA is indeed a regular political party, to be registered with the EC. But I hope the comparison with other parties, particularly the CCP, will end there. We are in the business to catalyse change. This is our principal aim. If that change encompasses a change to the government, then so be it. What we are not here for is to grab power by any means. No doubt we do seek power, but it is only to actualise the latent talent of the people, ensure poverty eradication and engender an economically free and culturally vibrant India. We will not hesitate to fight on issues that we feel are important to the nation – corruption in places high and low. Issues of public interest, like crony capitalism, crony socialism and excessive government intervention. Above all, we abhor the use of taxpayers' money for financing political nostrums and the party's future.

"Witness the current poorly crafted and targeted 'welfare schemes'. One can clearly see that these are for the welfare of the ruling clique and do little or no good to the people at large, much less the intended, 'poor' beneficiaries; who of course always remain 'poor'. Oh, how very kind! If you could just stop taxing us to death and let us keep our money, we can look after ourselves very well, thank you. Then of course we won't need you at all would we?

"Therein lies the rub. When we say taxation, we include the tax of inflation, which, incidentally, hits the poor the hardest. For, after all, if there are fewer poor people, maybe the ruling clique fears they will have that much fewer people to vote for them! Thus, behind all the earnest protestations and bleeding heart philosophy, there lies a rotten truth. The truth that the ruling clique keeps the people poor in order to stay in power. After all these years in office, this practice has been elevated to a fine art. We are bled even without being aware of it! I will take questions now." Ajit, after a sleepless night, felt tired and knew he looked it. The decision to quit the BGP and start a new party had been the most agonising and difficult decision in his life.

"Sir, reports suggest that many from the BGP are joining you. Is this correct? How do you think the BGP is going to react?"

"All I can say at the moment is that I have left the party only because I felt there were genuine differences of opinion on the direction the country should take. As for BGP workers joining me in the new party, that should not surprise anyone, as they have toiled selflessly for the goals I have outlined these past years. I take this opportunity to appeal to all right thinking people to join us, to be a part of the family of Jan Awaaz. Raise your for voice for the future of India. Today, we are at a critical crossroads. Our country's wellbeing rests on the capable shoulders of many of the young people I know are watching this telecast. I appeal to all of you – cast off your reticence, speak up for the nation. Cast off your apprehension about politics. I can promise you that we will be clean and transparent. Cast off your indolence –Mother India needs you! Professionals, IT specialists, journalists, skilled workers, unskilled workers, please come to us. We need you all to build the India of our dreams – where no one goes to bed hungry, no individual's liberty is abridged, and no person's innate ability goes waste. Come and join us. Let us make history together. Remember, I may be the convener of the party, but I am still just a worker. In this new party, whether you are president, general secretary or divisional secretary, we consider everyone as workers only. We invite everybody to discharge their duties to Mother India. You can contribute in the area of your specialisation.

"Join our program to eradicate corruption, and to reform procedures so that there is no going back to the bad old system. Join us to bring about ease of living and ease of livelihood to the many millions of people of this country. Our motto is 'That government is best which governs least', as Mahatma Gandhi advised us."

To Paresh, these developments gave his thoughts a new direction. He made a resolution then and there to join the JA and contribute to the election campaign.

It was early November, and Palam airport was covered in a thick cloak of fog. When Padamji looked out of the window of the British Airways flight from London, he was hardly able to see the wings of the aircraft. It was 7 in the morning, and the sun was taking its own time to show up. Winter was approaching, yet Padamji felt hot. Ajit's decision had forced him to revise his own plans. From all published reports, and through turncoats in his pay inside the BGP, he had been assured that Lalwani would be nominated again as PM candidate. This had suited him perfectly. Lalwani was a known player and a person of the old school, a member of the dwindling band of public figures to survive from the time of Independence. Like many of his peers, however hard he might fight against the CCP, there was an invisible line he would not cross. He would not hit so hard that the CCP broke up or suffered deep damage. Lalwani still clung to the romantic idea that the CCP was necessary for the unity of the country. Padamji smiled to himself – this was a lesson that had been drilled into him by the elders in his family.

Ajit was not like that. He was aggressive, spoke his mind and owned his decisions. Padamji knew that he hated the CCP and would do everything in his power to destroy the party. What was annoying and terrifying at the same time, was that Ajit would act politically, not violently on the streets. Padamji had been singed by his fire earlier. A single misstep could spell ruin. There was no doubt that if he could, Ajit would damage the CCP beyond repair.

This brought him to another dilemma. For the last four-and-a-half years, he had managed the government by appointing his trusted aide Shravan Verma as PM. Verma was an Oxbridge product. He was as obedient to Padamji as a poodle, and equally insipid as a personality. This suited Padamji very well. Naturally and logically, Padamji managed to appropriate for himself all the credit for things that were appreciated by the people while deftly pushing the blame on to Verma for any failures. Padamji did not care whether the policies his party and government followed were really for the benefit of the nation. He was satisfied if they kept him in power. Or rather, in control, but not in power; authority but not responsibility. This particular doctrine was the brainchild of his late mother.

Ajit's surprise decision had robbed Padamji of his comfort zone. From the tightening of his stomach, Padamji realised that he had a fight on his hands, against a cool, calculating and ruthless foe. There would be no room for mistakes. It was a 'winner takes all' –and God help the loser.

He went to the palatial building in Lutyens Delhi that he called home. He quickly showered and changed into a soft white pajama and a crisp, light brown kurta. This dress, though simple, was designed by Shraddha Kapoor, the only designer of international renown that Delhi could boast of. Breakfast was simple too – a couple of idlis and a cup of coffee. This was the only time he drank coffee. It would be tea up to six in the evening, after which he would hardly touch anything other than the best produce of Scotland.

He gave his wife a wave as he got into the ambassador car that was waiting to take him to the party's headquarters. For the first time in many years, he was prepared to listen to advice at the meeting he had called of his close comrades.

Chapter IX

Within a week, the JA had a website up and running. One of the first to volunteer was Paresh. All important announcements were made on the site in addition to usual media channels. Ajit clearly recognised that the increasing numbers of youth who had access to the Internet would play a big role in the party's and nation's future. To interact personally with volunteers like Paresh, the JA announced that it would conduct a three-day camp at Ranikhet. Anybody could apply to join the workshop. The number of people, personally chosen by Ajit, was limited to a hundred. The press dubbed them the 'JA Hundred'. The group consisted of mostly young men and women in their 30sand 40s; a handful were in their 20s, like Paresh. Ajit's aim was to give these technically qualified, professionally experienced people a taste of politics. He hoped that these promising youngsters would use their talent to power the party into the future. Thus, even as the party was being formed, Ajit was already thinking of the next generation. Paresh felt very proud to be associated with such a leader.

He was thrilled at being accepted and called to Ranikhet. He went through all the travel formalities with the enthusiasm and excitement of a teenager about to go on a holiday. As he waited for the approval for his credit card transaction, he wondered if Divya had been invited. He knew she was appreciative of Ajit; yet, did that also mean that she would volunteer for the JA? If she did, would she be compromising on her professional integrity as a journalist? Or, could she go in her capacity as a journalist? Wouldn't that be natural? Paresh wished he could ask her.

The meeting had been arranged at a resort just outside the town. The first meeting was scheduled to begin at 4 p.m., in a shamiana capable of accommodating several hundred people. Paresh who had arrived with the group earlier that day was disappointed at not meeting Ajit at lunch. As the sun sank behind the Himalayan peaks, Paresh found himself sitting in a plastic chair wishing the meeting would start. It was already past 4, according to the clock in his mobile.

Paresh had expected busy office bearers rushing about the place, while guards watched with hawk eyes for unwanted intruders. But Ajit's meeting failed to meet Paresh's expectation in this respect. People went about their work quietly. In fact, quite a few seemed to have nothing to do and lounged around, obviously gossiping. Others, who were not familiar with each other, looked on in silence. There were hardly any guards except for a bored policeman who seemed keener on getting the samosas and tea that were handed out from time to time than in exerting himself in the direction of 'being on guard' or anything in that line.

Apart from the said 'Hundred', Paresh discovered that there were many party officials from all over the country. He was not sure he wanted to attend a regular political meeting just yet. Paresh began to wonder whether he had done the right thing by volunteering. Quite bewildered by now with the lack of action, Paresh cast searching looks around, hoping that someone or the other would give some indication of acknowledging his existence, thus allowing him to start a conversation. Out of sheer boredom he decided to explore the premises. He walked slowly to the opening at end of the enclosure. He stepped out to face a steep set of steps cut into the rock. It was a hard climb. Nevertheless his frustration was so great that he would have gladly agreed to climb Nanda Devi if anybody had offered him the choice.

The climb was worth the trouble. Standing on the top of a small plateau at the back of a lush green lawn, the heritage building, framed by the snowy Himalayan peaks, was breathtakingly beautiful. It was white in colour, crowned with a sloping roof made of bright red tiles; and the undulating plastering revealed its British vintage. A verandah charmingly cloaked in climbing plants, ran along the front of building. As Paresh walked up the stone flagged path that divided the lawn equally, he felt himself transported back into the 19th century. Paresh stood for a moment, admiring the beautiful scene, then climbed the steps to the heavy beige door that was ajar.

In the days when he planned on making the trip there had been several scenarios that Paresh had envisioned on meeting Ajit. His favourite was something like this. When he met Ajit, Paresh would thrust his shoulders back, take a step forward, grasp Ajit's hand in a firm grip and say "Hello, how do you do? I am Paresh." Since he felt this was too common an approach, he rehearsed several openings; but none were satisfactory. They were either too informal – for example, "Hey brother! Nice to see you." This of course precluded a handshake and needed a high five. But would Ajit even reciprocate? Paresh felt he might not. So finally he decided on a formal handshake, accompanied by, "Hello Mr. Ajit. Great to meet you." That Paresh felt was neither too formal nor informal, and while sounding cosmopolitan, had the added advantage of the infusing in the proposed exchange, the vigour of youth.

The other scenario was the meeting with Divya, should she be present at Ranikhet. Paresh had rehearsed this meeting in his imagination a hundred times. He was confident of handling the situation perfectly, making the best impression he could. Unlike many youngsters, who spend hours before mirrors getting their opening lines correct, he elected to be guided by spontaneity where words were concerned. He would make contact with her eyes, even as a warm smile extended from his lips and lit up his dark eyes. He would then effortlessly greet her impressing her with both his sophistication and his moderation and not least of all his proud and regal bearing.

But neither of the above scenarios prepared Paresh for what happened next.

He stepped in and found the lobby empty. There was another door directly opposite. This led to a small room that had a musty smell, as though the windows had not been opened in a long time. There was another door directly ahead. Paresh doubted that he would find anything on the other side. He moved casually forward and gripped the handle when to his surprise it turned as though of its own volition. He was still gaping, as the door opened abruptly and nearly knocked his nose off. Surprised, he staggered back. His jaw dropped when a pretty young girl stepped in and looked at him inquiringly. Behind her loomed Ajit. It was too much of a surprise for Paresh to handle.

"Divya," he blurted out. Divya just stared back at him. Obviously, she did not like the way things were going.

"Yes," she said sharply, a frown marring her beautiful face.

"I thought you weren't coming!"

She did not reply but the flash in her eyes said all that was necessary. Paresh's face burned. He knew he owed her an apology, even though he couldn't help feeling that there was no need for that momentary anger on her part.

Before he could make amends, Ajit, along with half a dozen of his party members, walked into the room.

"I..." was all that Paresh had time to utter.

"Let's go to the meeting hall. We can talk there." Ajit said in a business-like tone and pulled Paresh gently around by his elbow, forcing him to turn and fall into step with Ajit. The very fact that he walking in step with Ajit took Paresh's breath away. Something solid kept coming up his throat, which failed to go down, however many times he tried to swallow it. He was so engrossed in the developments that they reached the hall by the time Paresh found his voice. By then, it was too late to say anything – the people had started to gather around Ajit.

Paresh found himself quickly surrounded by burly men in white kurtas and pajamas and cream-coloured Nehru jackets. They stepped forward strongly into the crowd, urging the people to quieten down, even as they escorted Ajit to a small dais in the centre of one side of the enclosure.

After some polite exchanges with the people about politics, Ajit announced in a loud voice that he would like to discuss important economic issues. He invited questions.

"You say that you will tax luxury products at the same rates as for widely used products. Isn't this inherently unfair? Why should the rich not be made to pay more for their luxuries?" A young man in a red shirt and gargoyle glasses wanted to know.

Ajit considered the question for a minute. He cleared his throat before speaking. "What is a luxury product?"

The man's face became immobile, as if, behind those glasses, some rusty machinery attempted to work.

"Something that the rich buy out of arrogance, even if there is no need for it." Appearances could be deceptive – Paresh would never have credited the man with such a cogent statement.

"Well," Ajit frowned. "Let's say that a rich man buys a Benz car. This is manufactured by many people, none of whom are millionaires. Agreed?" The man nodded.

"Then the car has to be transported, financed, serviced and repaired. All these tasks are performed by ordinary people. What they have is employment, a job. A job that adds value, and for which someone is willing to compensate them. Thus, even a so-called luxury product creates many jobs. It is by doing these jobs that the poor can improve their own standards of living. That is why I am opposed to the so-called 'sin' taxes. Such taxes on energy, say petrol at least makes some sense in terms of protecting the environment, but otherwise, I am afraid such policies will simply end up stultifying industrial enterprise."

"The government itself can give jobs by implementing employment guarantee programs."

"You are right. The government can indeed provide guaranteed employment. The question then arises: How and from where does the government get its revenues?"

"From the rich." The red shirt interrupted Ajit triumphantly.

"Quite right. But where do the rich get their so-called riches from?" The question, rhetorical as it was, seemed to have stumped the man, for he attempted no answer. "Simple! It is no secret that most rich people become that way by selling goods and services to poor and ordinary people. Thus, if you tax them heavily, at least some if not all the tax burden would be passed on to the consumer. A tax seemingly on the rich, actually prevents the poor from buying and enjoying goods and services, which, but for the high taxes, they would have been able to afford. A classic example is the air-conditioner or refrigerator. A high tax on these so-called luxury goods means that these goods are priced beyond the reach of the common man. Not only that, all the jobs that would be available in transporting and repairing and servicing these machines, skills that can be easily learnt by the poorest of the poor are lost. What is seen is a high tax on a luxury product appreciated as a tax to curb the rich and make 'resources' available for the poor. What is not seen are the thousands of jobs that are lost as a result."

The man now thought it prudent to put up his hand before speaking. "But government programmes provide work and sustenance to impoverished people. This can only help the economy."

"Only if the work is fully productive. If the creation of jobs means digging some ditches and then filling them back again, or if wages are paid just for attendance while actually nothing gets done, then, far from any development taking place, it would lead to inflationary conditions. Frederic Bastiat, the French savant, gave the illustration of the broken windows. If windows are broken, then workmen get work by repairing these windows. So in a town, if, say, the windows of all houses are broken in a round robin fashion, then these workers would have work all year round. This is true as far as the workers go. But, when you analyse it a little more deeply, you will notice that merely repairing windows broken for that very purpose hardly adds to the wellbeing of the community. This is how all welfare employment measures work. What is actually needed is production of new goods and services.

"Don't mistake me. These measures are okay for the short term, or in the face of some great economic calamity. Such calamities can happen to entire nations or even the whole world as during the Great Depression. But more often, it happens in individual peoples' lives. For instance, you lose a job and you need work to keep body and soul together. In such circumstances, and for those people, I am sure these jobs, any job at all, would be a great blessing. So, such policies may be continued; but continuance as a matter of routine in a wholesale fashion is detrimental to the long-term prospects of the economy."

Paresh raised his hand. "You talk about liberalism and libertarianism. There is one criticism that there is nothing in our history that encourages individual action. In fact, these critics go on to argue that, even now, elections are being won only on caste and communal grounds, both of which are collectives." Paresh wiped his forehead as he sat down.

Ajit looked carefully at Paresh. "That a very good question. Your name, sir?"

"Paresh."

"Thanks Paresh, for raising this important point. Now I know this is an argument that has been advanced by several people. However I think of it as being too clever by half. What literature exists in India, or for that matter, any literature in the world, for collectivism? The base, nearly always, has been the *Das Kapital* of Marx. And this tome was written by an individual acting individually, sitting in a country that was foreign to his own. Let us not forget this. No Planning Commission or State Committee on Ideology mandated this work – this book, which has had such a large influence on human thinking, and, more unfortunately, on human lives. Thus, the argument that collectivist ideas also have no basis in Indian literature too should hold good.

"Coming back to the criticism of there being no emphasis on the individual in India, I pose this simple question: Do our texts say that we will go to swarg or narag along with our other caste members or even with our family members? Sounds stupid, doesn't it? On the other hand, our texts lay emphasis on individual action, tapas, adhering to satya and dharma to advance our spiritual cause. Actually, whenever you perform rituals it is customary to end by saying, 'No, this is not for me'. The reason is that by giving up the merit such actions carry, we are in fact ensuring our own future in the after-life. And don't ask me if such things exist – that is a completely different discussion. Let us go on with what our practises are and what our texts say.

"Thus, we perform actions to secure a good future, realising at the same time the smallness of the 'I' involved in doing it. This, I would say, is a sterling example of enlightened self-interest. So, while we may all identify ourselves with some group or other, our ultimate struggle, so to speak, has always been on the individual plane.

"Further, the *Artha Shastra* recognises the obligation of the king to promote trade agriculture and manufactures. Agriculture is given high importance. At the same time, it cautions the king on the tendency of his servants, the bureaucracy, to misappropriate finances. Clearly, many of the problems we face in modern public administration have been given deep thought more than 2,000 years ago. While it gives the State, or the king, a major role in the economy, Chanakya is very farsighted in stating that the precepts laid out were applicable for his time only. Other people could, and should, modify it to suit their own environments and times. This, then, is the basis for Indian Liberalism. In the here and now, it is a good idea." Ajit looked inquiringly at the audience for the next question.

Paresh saw Divya raise her hand. His heart thumped wildly. He wanted her to ask a really bright question. The strength of the feeling surprised him. "Sir, how about the extremism some people in your group exhibit? Be it women's clothing, lifestyle, equality for women, or the rights of minorities to practise their religions?"

"There are two things here. One is our historical tradition, primarily concerning women. The other is our Constitution, which guarantees everyone equality. Today, we stand at a place where we have been subjected to foreign rule and cultural influences for a thousand years or more. We cannot wish this legacy away. Whatever we do, if elected, will be within the framework of the constitution. As Kalidasa aptly put it many years ago, 'Not everything that is old is good, and not everything that is new is bad'. We must seek to strike a compromise between the good, the old, and the new. Let us keep whatever is good in our culture, let us part gently with whatever is bad. Let us not brush aside new ideas of cultural developments, still, let us remain rooted in our own culture. I personally think that what we must do is to adapt modern influences to our cultural moorings. For example, take Valentine's Day. This is a European custom. Can't we, amongst all our epics and literature, find some equivalent for this? Can't we then celebrate the equivalent of a Valentine's Day on that day? I am not saying that we must necessarily do so. This is a suggestion to those to object to such celebrations.

"My take on all such matters is we should re-examine the basis of new ideas, and, if we find them good, fit them into the cultural context. The only caveat is that the whole process must be free from use of force by either side."

"What is our foreign policy matrix? Will it be different from the non-aligned dogma we have followed from the 1950s?" This was from a chubby, bearded man in his mid-30s, who said his name was Shashank Chakraborti. Paresh sighed –another worthy son of Bengal, from JNU no doubt. The only surprise was that he was here at all.

"Our domestic policy is to put the economy above politics. Our foreign policy is to put the economy front and centre of diplomacy. We will pursue a policy that enhances our trading position, and we will strive to keep markets open, particularly for our cutting-edge IT services. We strongly believe in the International Division of Labour. Hence, we will pursue an open trade policy. There are some who advocate a unilateral free trade policy. However, I don't believe that, as a nation, we are ready to embrace such a radical step. We will negotiate trade deals with all countries while keeping national interests in view. However, we will definitely not close the doors to imports if they are cheaper and better than domestic manufactures. We want to encourage our domestic manufacturers to attain and maintain world-class standards. We will not choose sides. Our policy will be to let the industries fight it out in the market. We will favour to some extent the consumer over the industrialist.

"Jan Awaaz's policy is clear in this regard. Let me quote Kabir:

Kabira Khara Bazaar Mein, Mange Sabki Khair,
Na Kahu Se Dosti, Na Kahu Se Bair.

(Kabira in the market place, wishes welfare of all,
Neither friendship nor enmity with anyone at all.)

"Now and then, a cry is raised that we should be part of the Permanent Council at the UN. On this matter, I urge that we think more clearly. All of us are aware of how often the Big Five can be unjust, how they can pursue their own interests even to the detriment of others. The question is, if we believe that the Big Five system is inherently unfair, as it makes the five countries more equal than others, then what is the rationale behind demanding a seat for ourselves? Are we ready to be cursed by other countries that cannot enjoy that privilege? Will the stain of injustice of the system be simply washed away just because we join the Big Five?

"There are many sound arguments for the reform of the UN system. This subject must be pursued in a holistic manner, not just in terms of getting a permanent seat. I suggest that an international committee formed under the auspices of the UN can study this matter deeply. I think this may be the way out for an equitable world order."

Paresh had an exhilarating afternoon. They broke up for dinner while animated discussions went on. Soon, he realised that Chakraborti was an ardent anarcho-capitalist, whose main worry seemed to be that Ajit would not go far enough to liberate the individual Indian. "The first act, if we are voted to power, should be to restore property rights as a fundamental right, just as it was in the 1950 Constitution." Further, he spoke of unilateral free trade and a catallaxy of businessmen and women peacefully carrying on trade over and within borders. He also introduced Paresh to the lucid economic writings of B.R. Shenoy, who, Paresh learnt from Chakraborti, had correctly predicted the currency crisis of 1957-58 and the inflation that continuous deficit financing would entail. This was the famous Note of Dissent on the Second Plan. It was this piece that, despite being spot on in forecasting the deficiencies of the plan, led him to being shunted out of ruling circles. He then spent his days teaching at a university in Gujarat. So much for the vaunted liberalism and freedom of expression of that hypocritical age.

On the second day, Paresh finished his morning chores quickly, hoping to hit the breakfast table before the rest of the crowd did. If there was one thing he disliked in life, it was to be hurried through a meal. However, he found that food would not be served before 7.30. That left him with more than half-an-hour on his hands. He dismissed the thought of taking a walk about the place, as the weather was rather chilly. He went to the front of the heritage building. The resort property was tiered and the meeting room was on a lower level, reached by a flight of stairs. Adjacent to the meeting hall was the dining area. The food was cooked at a specially set up kitchen at a yet lower level that was not visible from where Paresh was standing. There were several cottages at lower levels reached by stepped pathways for easy descent. Climbing up the slope was another question altogether.

From the lawn on the plateau, one could see across the Himalayan ranges at Nanda Devi. There was a telescope, in name only, as Paresh had discovered the previous day, fixed on a stand on the boundary wall. Still, it offered a better view of the majestic mountain than could be had by the naked eye. He grasped the handle and put his eyes to the viewfinder. He soon became engrossed in rearranging the row of snow clad peaks –trying various permutations and combinations, all in his imagination only, to improve the look of the range. He soon concluded that he could not beat Mother Nature's creation. Just then, he heard a sound behind him, the touch of sandals on soft grass. Tearing his eyes away from the viewfinder, he saw Divya standing a few feet behind him, to his left. There were a couple of other people coming down from their rooms, also obviously waiting for breakfast to be served.

"Good morning," he said with a bright smile. She seemed to be in a reverie and took a moment before returning the greeting. She probably wished to be left alone at this time of the morning. Paresh carefully wiped the smile from his face even as he turned back to the telescope.

"Is that Nanda Devi?" Her voice energised him.

"Yes," Paresh responded quickly. "That one!" He stretched his arm towards the row of peaks. "That one there, which looks like a gymnastic horse, there at the back."

"Yes, I think I see it now. Can I use the telescope?"

"Of course." Paresh moved away, though he still held the handle. He bent his arm to let Divya look into the viewfinder, before releasing the handle to her.

"Thank you. I can see it very well from here. My gosh! It looks sublime, doesn't it? I mean the entire range and also the peak itself. I believe it has never been climbed."

"I don't know about that part," Paresh said. "But yes, it looks heavenly. No wonder our ancestors went into yonder mountains when they went looking for God."

"Yeah," breathed Divya. "That's remarkably well put. Hey, you know what? I think you should be a journalist." Paresh felt himself blushing. He desperately hoped, that Divya with her eyes still glued on the mountains, hadn't seen him.

Divya stepped back and stood up. Paresh decided that a change of subject was in order.

"I suppose you didn't find time to ask Padamji's media advisor about Ranjan?" His voice was diffident. Divya stared at him for a moment, visibly chagrined. "I am really very sorry..." she began. Her eyes glowed for a brief moment. "Paresh?"

Paresh nodded.

"What with all the excitement of the last few weeks, I forgot completely about it." She sounded apologetic. He waved his hand and shook his head, indicating that it did not matter. "Anyway, I did call Ajay, Deb's assistant.Deb is Padamji's press advisor."

"Can't you ask Deb himself?"

She gave a short laugh, but it sounded more like a bark to Paresh. "You can't approach Deb with such things. I will speak to Ajay again and see what he has to say. Personally I think you may be right about that angle." This was enough for Paresh– his day was made.

The morning session was devoted to articulating of the party's policies by Ajit. The method adopted was that Ajit would put forth prescriptions. The group would first vote on it. Then based on whether or not it found favour with the group, it would be discussed. The logic behind this strange method was that if it found favour it would be further fine-tuned and adopted as a party policy. If an idea was rejected initially by the group, it would tell Ajit and his team two things – one, that it was likely to be equally unpopular with the masses, and, secondly, that it would have to be clarified and developed further. If the revised version was voted for favourably, then, that too, would make it to the party platform.

"No clear change can take place if we continue to traverse the present path of 'taking along' the oldies and rule bound leaders," Ajit said. "What we need is an ideology of liberty and a crew of street-smart fighters, at home equally in the crowded malodorous jhompidis as well as in the plush drawing rooms of south Delhi. The key is ideology. Mahatma Gandhi spoke not only of change but of the importance of the quality of the means to that change. If the means were faulty, then the real benefits of change, whatever its nature cannot be enjoyed. The Mahatma advised his followers to practise what they preached – 'Be the change you want to see,' he urged them."

Practically every hand went up for this proposition. Ajit smiled. "I think we have something like hundred percent consensus on this.

"In the new millennium, we must develop an all-encompassing political machine that would carry all with it. The ideology that I put forth is not mindless selfishness, it is not even enlightened self interest. I want to go beyond these concepts. I say the while we must be aware of our interests we must be equally sensitive to the interests of others, since these affect our interests directly. Hence we must balance the liberty to pursue our aims with fraternal feelings for others interests.

"India has done well to foster, nurture and preserve a free polity. Now, as we grapple with a fast-changing world and a rapidly morphing demographic, we need to get our economic act right. This can best be provided by a free economy. Thus, the answer to the present-day ills, mainly corruption, social injustice, inequality in income, poor health and education parameters all have deep roots in the collectivist nature of the Indian economy. JA proposes to change this by appealing to people in all walks of life to embrace individual liberty and autonomy in decision-making. Excesses of a 'free' economy would be 'naturally' restrained by the operation of an equally 'free' polity. Vice versa, the practise of a free polity would provide the basis for consistency, transparency and continuity in economic policies, leading to near ideal conditions." Again, most hands went up. They would, thought Paresh; the group consisted mostly of likeminded people.

"'Economic freedom is the heart of freedom,' Rajaji said. Under conditions of economic freedom, as a consumer – and we are all consumers –each person exercises his or her freedom of choice every day. When a person offers to sell and another agrees to buy, we have a 'market'. It is a catallaxy, or as Freidrich Von Hayek described it; 'the order brought about by the mutual adjustment of many individual economies in a market'." This time only about half the hands went up. Paresh who had his hand up was dismayed to note that Divya's hand was firmly on her lap.

Ajit nodded in acknowledgement and continued.

"By the term market, I do not mean or in any way imply that it exists or should exist only for some big businessmen or the well to do sections of the middle-class. For me it covers all sections of society. Recently, I was in Chennai. There, near the wine shops, many old women were selling pickles. This is a form of spontaneous entrepreneurship. Ethics behind the sale of alcohol is a debate for another day. This is just one example of the spirit of enterprise of our people, even the most humble of them. My intention is to create the conditions and the laws and the infrastructure to multiply career opportunities for all Indians.

"In this context, let me take the example of the one-rupee shampoo sachet. A young man realised that practically all shampoos in the market were delivered in package sizes that put them out of reach of the poorest, which actually constituted about 50% of the market by population though less in monetary terms. The new company solved the packing and logistical problems and began selling shampoo in one-rupee packets. This helped create a new market, and even the poorest of the poor started to use shampoo. Hitherto, they had to content themselves with merely watching others use shampoo, while they continued with the traditional shikakkai.

"This had a domino effect in the market. Not only did other cosmetic product businesses scramble to produce similar products, the concept travelled to other goods too. For example, biscuit manufactures put out five-rupee packets – the minimum prices till then had been double that. The same went for many other products such as hair oil. The most obvious thing about the above narration is that this consumer revolution was not produced by the Planning Commission or any of the other of the tens of committees of 'experts' who toil day and night to 'advise' the government. A socially useful and economically satisfying move was made by an individual acting in his individual capacity, seeking gain for himself, while serving a section of consumers; in this case the poorest of the poor. This is a good case of 'corporate social responsibility'.

"This, then, is the real power of the market where people aim to serve other people. When you do this, naturally you have to employ people, and pay them wages and salaries. You have to provide for upgrading your machines, organisation, selling your products, and finally, you have to take care of yourself. Otherwise, you would not be able to serve the market. This, in other words, is what economists call employment, depreciation, marketing and brand building, and profit. Profit is not only an incentive to serve the market – it also provides the resources for the next round of investment."

This time all the hands were up except for the man in red wearing gargoyle glasses.

The dialogue continued on the third day. "A National Social Welfare Fund would be created," Ajit said. "This general fund would be available to all citizens. The central government's share of revenues from auction or lease of natural resources would be credited to this account instead of the general budget. A portion of the indirect taxes, on goods and services, including excise, and customs would also be credited to this fund. A lesser portion of direct taxes would also find its way into this account. The amount in this fund would be used for welfare payments to the poor. The poor would be identified with existing, well-established methodologies. These changes would be carried out over three or four budgets, to ensure minimum disruption during the changeover period. Existing social welfare programs would be thoroughly scrutinised and expenditure would be progressively debited to this fund instead of the general budget. Welfare-related expenses, including those that are incurred by the states would be met from this account. The public would also be allowed to make tax-deductible contributions to this fund.

"The aim of this fund would be to assess the genuine welfare needs of the society and identify revenue sources to meet the same. In this system, there could be no deficit under this account – this will keep a check on the tendency of political parties to throw money at schemes, which, while masquerading as welfare initiatives, are actually electoral bribes to specific constituencies. It is hoped that once this system becomes operational, the ruling clique, to whichever party it might belong, would no longer be able to use taxpayers' money to ensure its re-election.

"While government agencies would be used primarily to deliver the welfare measures to the public, we will introduce a system of 'marketing' as well. The attempt is to 'productise' social welfare, so that it can be marketed through private citizens, such as NSC and LIC agents. For example, if a person wants a ration card, he/she has to go to a government department, stand in queue and give 'something' before he/she gets anything, if at all. What we propose is that a person seeking welfare would simply call or approach an accredited agent. This agent would verify the credentials of the person who is to receive welfare and pass it on to the concerned department for further action. The department can then process these papers, calling the intended beneficiary only in case of doubt. Once the papers are processed, the welfare measure, whatever it may be, would be directly delivered to the person asking for it. The agent would receive a commission for the facilitation."

Most people agreed with this proposal.

"The second major social welfare plan would be to create a National Labour Fund. This would consist of a portion of direct and indirect taxes, but not revenues from national resources. Further, both employers and employees would also contribute to this fund in the same manner as they do now for Provident Fund.

"In fact, the system of PF and pension would be completely recast. All workers would be covered by a national pension system, with several alternative schemes to choose from. There will be different schemes for maximum capital accrual, or the highest monthly amount possible. Each company and its unions or unions would have to agree to the scheme. The whole thing would be voluntary. Companies that sign on would be able to hire and fire. A national online employment exchange would be created to help such displaced workers to find new jobs. This would be twinned with retraining programmes funded by the government. Monthly payments would be made to workers for the duration of their unemployment, subject to reasonable restrictions. Companies would contribute towards unemployment insurance and residence transfer expenses. A part of the cost would be underwritten from the National Labour Fund. This scheme would also assure workers of job security for themselves and education security for their children. Unions would also help find other jobs for such displaced members. Labour unions would become partly like HR firms."

Fewer than before voted for this proposal. Ajit agreed to refine these ideas before incorporation in the manifesto.

"There is already legislation for providing guaranteed employment. We would take this forward and club it with our proposal for unemployment insurance. A corollary would be that the Minimum Wages Act would become redundant if a state-sponsored employment guarantee is there. The obvious advantage is that, in general, nobody would go for employment below the rates paid under this scheme, but if someone wants to take a job at a lower wage, he/she would be free to do so, unlike at present. This would give them vital work experience that they can leverage for higher paying jobs. This is expected to largely eliminate under-employment as well as the phenomenon of the unemployables.

"A minimum tax on goods and services would be imposed to cover vocational education and for retraining unemployed people under the above scheme. Income and corporate taxes would fund the general budget, which would include 'normal' activities expected from any government, such as police, defence, courts and normal oversight functions including regulatory authorities.

"This system of clearly segregated income and expense heads would ensure transparency in accounting government revenues and expenses. Wealth tax would be abolished as would capital gains tax. Income tax would be applicable only to those earning rupees 10 lakhs or more. Corporate taxes would be cut to 15%; in the bargain, there will be no deductions and concessions. All incomes including export incomes would be taxable. There will be a 10% surcharge on corporate taxes, which would go directly to a National Defence Fund. So too for GST, which will go to the National Social Welfare Fund. Simplicity of tax structure and transparency in assessment procedures should ensure revenue buoyancy.

"Foreign investors would be able to invest 49% in any business venture automatically. Further investments would be cleared by a Foreign Investment Board on a case-by-case basis. Decisions would have to be made in 90 days and clear reasons will be given for rejections and acceptances. This is most important because, every time a proposal is accepted, that would be a ratification of our policies; a statement on rejection would reinforce policy essentials."

The main takeaway for Paresh from the meeting was that he was doing something for the country at last. He felt very proud and a warm sensation of wellbeing washed over him. All in all, he returned to Bangalore a satisfied man, and a firm friend of Divya's. The trip had been very pleasant. The air was indeed pure as the cliché went, and Ranikhet lived up to its billing of being an unspoiled piece of Himalayan landscape. The green valleys were soothing to the eye, just as the white peaks were a balm to the tired mind.

For Divya, the trip had been too short. She was a people-person and she was confident in her ability to judge people quickly, often on the spot. She wished it had gone on for longer than the three days. Maybe a week or 10 days. She could have got to know those present much better. There had been many impressive people at the meet, many of them well known. Yet, on thinking further, she found that she had spent most of her time with two of them.

Chakraborti was intellectually very impressive –his knowledge of economic, political and social theories was fantastic. What made him even more attractive for Divya was that he was fun too.

Paresh was different. With his cheerful smile, the no-nonsense look, and firm handshake, Paresh had impressed her. She always responded to human warmth. Basically from the middle-class, like herself, he was a sober man, the kind who got things done. In a crisis, he would be the one she would like to have around her. He was good looking too, and took care to keep fit. This was one of Divya's pet peeves – she hated flab, especially on youngsters. It told her that they were both careless about their bodies and too lazy to do something about it. She had never liked those who drank too much, were clearly rich and definitely arrogant. Paresh had clean-cut features, a firm body and an open manner. She was glad that she had befriended him, not just on Facebook but face-to-face as well. She hoped that their friendship would develop and continue for years to come. All this musing reminded her of Paresh's request. She called Ajay to find out if some secret deal had been struck between Padamji and Ranjan.

Ajay is not forthcoming and I can't ask directly, Divya wrote to Paresh. *So I asked him for his opinion about Ranjan being in touch with Padamji. He seemed to be taken aback a bit. I think he decided to say nothing, fearing that he would be provoked into making an undesirable public admission. Being the good guy that he is, he has promised to revert as soon as he has some information. So, you can be happy that your theory is most likely right – else Ajay would not have reacted the way he did.*

Paresh was thrilled that Divya was communicating with him, even if it was only over email. Not that he did not care about Ranjan or Padamji, just that it seemed far less important than chatting and exchanging mails with Divya. Yet, this time around, it was Paresh who lost track of this particular conversation. Elections were nearing and the political scene was starting to heat up.

Chapter X

On a cold Thursday morning, Divya was just finishing breakfast when Ajay called.

"Padamji wants you to tell Kiran to prepare for an interview with him." Divya was taken aback. She had expected Ajay to call about Ranjan. Why would Padamji want her to tell Kiran when he could just as easily ask Ajay to do so? Since when was a journalist told to 'prepare' for an interview? Was this a hoax, an effort to pull her leg? On second thoughts, she knew Ajay reasonably well and was sure that he would not pull such tricks on her.

"Why me and not you? I mean you could call Kiran yourself rather than have me tell her," she added hastily.

Ajay laughed. "For that, you would have to ask Padamji himself. I am merely following instructions."

Divya was now afraid that Kiran would think she was getting above herself.

"Kiran won't like this." Her chest was tight and she had to make an effort just to breathe. She wondered if she would lose her job.

"Why so?"

"I mean, she may think that I bypassed her..."

"No chance at all." Ajay interrupted her. "Just tell her that this message is from Padamji. She will understand."

A thought struck Divya.

"Is there truth in the rumour that she had had an affair with Padamji?" Divya wished she had not asked that question. Ajay's reply was as indirect as it was full of meaning: "Small people like us should not ask such questions." He hung up.

So, the rumours were true. Divya shuddered involuntarily. She couldn't bring herself to think that Kiran, who had been so nice to her, was that sort of woman. Divya prided herself on being modern, but did not consider such mercenary behaviour either modern or in good taste. After a few more tumultuous minutes, she calmed down. This was the way of the world, at least in 21st century India.

She would share her feelings with Paresh but not immediately. Her first task was to deal with the journalistic coup that had been handed to her. She was a realist who saw that she had done little to deserve such a favour and couldn't yet understand why. However, from a professional point of view, she was very excited. To be singled out by Padamji was a rare honour, particularly for someone in her position. She could now expect her career to go places. Of that, she was sure. Once the word got around that she was one of his courtiers, many doors and big purses would be opened for her. She could look forward to a fulfilling career and good money–a combination any journalist would give their right hands for.

She wondered how Padamji even knew of her existence. Ajay must have spoken about her to his boss. How else would they even know of her existence? Divya felt angry.

She would confront Ajay on this but that would have to wait.

For now, she would bask in the glow that Padamji's unexpected invitation had placed her in. In her excitement, she did not stop to think about why he had specifically targeted her. She simply assumed that he had been impressed by her professional credentials. Young as she was, it never occurred to her that the innocuous invitation could imply a sinister design.

She called Kiran to tell her of the news. Then she sent an SMS to her mother. She wouldn't tell anyone else, including her closest friends. Unaccountably, she felt guilty about not letting Paresh know of her good fortune.

Padamji agreed to be interviewed at his home, a privilege rarely granted. Not even Tony Rai had managed to get an interview with Padamji at his residence. This impressed Divya very much, and she threw herself headlong into preparing for the interview. There was not much to research, but there was much to do, particularly in terms of optics. Visuals were as important as the words that would be spoken. Maybe even more. Kiran insisted on grand dresses for herself and Divya – at the company's cost, of course.

Divya reached Padamji's house by 8a.m., even though the interview was only at twelve. Everything that the camera could capture was important. This was insisted on by Padamji and agreed to by Kiran. She came a little later and went straight upstairs to Padamji's bedroom, to descend only at a quarter to twelve. Divya did feel that this was strange, but nobody else said anything about it. Maybe this was how the heady high society represented by Padamji functioned.

Kiran Butt's interview with Padamji was held in the bigger drawing room of his enormous government bungalow. There was a big sofa on the longer side of the oblong room, while an ornately carved stand was placed on the narrow side. Opposite the big sofa were a couple of plush sofas in front of a French window. The windows were covered with an intricately worked fabric curtain. Overhead was a fine chandelier and a thick and obviously expensive carpet covered the entire floor. Divya felt like she was in the private quarters of a maharaja, before she realised that Padamji was indeed one, even though the system had the facade of a democracy.

The cameraman asked her to take a view before finalising the camera position. Divya crossed the room noiselessly, her medium heels sinking disconcertingly in the carpet. The view of the sofa and the greenery beyond the French windows was good. She turned her attention to the list of questions to be asked.

Soon, Padamji and Kiran came down. He stopped to look at Divya, who found herself blushing under his gaze. "Hey Kiran, who is your pretty friend?"

"Divya Rao," Kiran said. Padamji shook Divya's hands and bowed slightly. His grip on her hand was firm, and he looked at her in a manner that could only be called a leer. Divya tried to pull her hand away; she was sure that everyone else was staring at them. He smiled and released her hand. Divya looked around and was quite relieved to find that not one person was looking in their direction. Not even Kiran Butt, who was now carefully adjusting her top.

"We must have tea together one of these days." Padamji's voice was like a caress. Divya was too surprised to do more than nod her head. In her mind, she was clear that she would refuse when such an invitation actually materialised.

He gave her a friendly wave, which apparently covered Kiran as well, before sinking into the soft embrace of the plush sofa. Kiran sat in another sofa at a right angle. Padamji beamed genially at everyone. He smiled and everyone gushed, Divya noted, her cheeks reddening as he looked directly at her with the warmest smile anyone had received from him.

Then, in a clear if soft voice, he asked Kiran to start the interview. Divya was standing behind Kiran such that she would not be in the angle of the camera. For the next hour, she would only be a spectator as the interview was filmed. But she was exceedingly uncomfortable as Padamji kept looking at her from time to time. He seemed to be oblivious of cameramen, light boys and others. It was a very embarrassing hour for Divya.

On the one hand, she was thrilled that an important person like Padamji had cared to spare a glance for her; on the other, she felt uncomfortable with Padamji's strange behaviour. Adding to her troubles was the fact that whenever she found herself under Padamji's gaze, Paresh's face kept coming up before her eyes. And this, she did not understand at all.

The interview itself was something of a damp squib, in Divya's opinion. She felt that there was no need for Kiran to be so soft in her questioning. Neither was it becoming of a nationally acclaimed journalist to blush just so much when looking at Padamji. Kiran did ask some relevant question on inflation, the economic downturn, political alignments and such, but she seemed to be overawed, even deferential to

Padamji. Kiran's questions seemed both perverse and totally lacking in context. This was surprising to Divya, who knew how aggressive Kiran could be. She recalled the interview with Ajit three months earlier.

"I suppose peace with Pakistan could have been possible if your dad and then Pakistan PM Jahanara Khan had married," Kiran asked in a coquettish tone.

"Yes, yes, they got on very well. But for interference from Rawalpindi, they would have sewn up a historic peace pact then and there."

Chapter XI

Paresh took a sabbatical at the beginning of February, since elections were due in about three months. He would move to Delhi to assist JA.

The first thing he did was to call Divya. For him, two major faultlines were intersecting each other – his obsession with Divya and his interest in working for a better country. When he went to Delhi, there would be many opportunities to see Divya even as he worked for the JA. He could hardly contain his excitement.

"What would you have done if your boss had refused leave?" Divya did not seem to see eye to eye on this one.

"Simple. I would have quit."

"How can you be so casual about your job? I would not dare to think of quitting mine."

"Well, I haven't quit. Just took off."

"For three months?" Paresh did not miss the incredulity in her voice.

"I have worked 24/7 for months together. Gone without a single day off, for weeks. Those things add up you know. Anyway if they refuse, I would just quit. I am sure my skill sets would be more than welcome in a dozen global companies."

"Arrogance!"

"Not at all," he said in a low voice. Just stating facts...as I see them." He wished he had not spoken so about himself.

"I really didn't mean that. But looks like you IT guys have all the fun." Her tone now matched his and he felt immeasurably better.

'*New Deal* for the poor! Padamji announces new schemes targeted at removing poverty in six years'. The news was splashed in bold letters across the front page. Paresh read the headline with a sinking sensation in his stomach. For Paresh, the victory of the JA and Ajit was, by now, a personal matter. Had Padamji, the cunning political fox that he was, already turned the tables on Ajit and the JA? This question agitated Paresh so much that he could not read through the full news report. He put the paper aside. His normally rational mind felt as though it was made of rock. However much he tried to cajole it to think, it refused to budge. This was something new – he had never felt like this before. It was not panic that afflicted him, just a seeming incapacity to get his brain moving. He took a deep breath, went to the fridge and drank some cold water. He then forced his unwilling mind and body to do the daily chores that his new location demanded. He now shared a room with Chakraborti at a JA supporter's house in Patel Nagar, New Delhi.

The JA's war room, where the details were discussed and from which a veritable army of young professionals supported the critical communications centre, was just down the road. Paresh was on the IT support team, which had the responsibility of maintaining JA's website. He found it difficult to concentrate and, by forenoon, a strong sense of depression took hold of him. His feelings needed an outlet, someone to talk to. His thought of Divya, but he knew that while talking to her would make him forget the present, it was the future he was worried about now. He shuddered at the thought of the CCP winning again. From the way the new schemes were being reported, it looked as though the JA could be written off then and there. He would have to wait until Chakraborti, who had gone out on some fieldwork, returned. He hoped that Chakraborti's firm grip on economics would illuminate the situation as it existed.

Later that evening settled comfortably in a cane armchair and nursing a cold beer, Paresh put the question foremost in his mind to Chakraborti. "Did you see this morning's headlines? Think Padamji can pull it off?"

"Hardly," was Chakraborti's reply to Paresh's anxious question. "Firstly, the government does not have the money to finance the new schemes. Secondly, the budget deficit is high and all revenues will have to be spent on reducing it. Thirdly, with inflation also running high –a natural corollary of high fiscal deficits– the government dare not pump any more money into the economy. Anyway, if you look closely at the schemes, one wonders if they are at all meant for implementing. All this noise and drama seems to be aimed at making news and headlines, with little to show on the ground. Take, for instance, the food scheme. Can you imagine a Tata or a Birla needing food security?

"Leave alone such people. A large part of the middle-class today is not looking for dole – they are looking for opportunities. When the tsunami hit in 2004, many people in Chennai collected used clothes and gave them to the fisher folk who had lost their homes. You know what they thought of this 'good' deed? They said, 'We are middle-class people, please do not give us old clothes. If possible, buy us new clothes, but please don't insult us with these hand-me-downs!' This is 21st century India for you."

Paresh began to feel better, but he was not fully reassured. He knew that many people still believed in the power of the 'good' that a government could do. Of course, there were many genuinely good things that a government could indeed do. For example, in education, in public health and, most importantly, in setting and enforcing standards. This was not the 'good' that worried Paresh. He was concerned about the giveaways that Padamji could shower on an unsuspecting electorate, using taxpayers' money.

Again, the real problem with supporting a free economy was that it was an easy target for politicians. How did one defend one's views politically?

"Although economic freedom is a good thing in itself, did it not also open the way for unscrupulous elements? Wouldn't the single-minded pursuit of profit, to the exclusion of all other factors, reduce human beings to mere statistical data points?"

"What about all the people who are forced to obtain ration cards from a bureaucracy that neither gives service nor is civil?"

"Don't get worked up," Paresh said, smiling. "I am just asking a question that CCP may throw at us. In fact I know for a fact that a lot of people expect a lucid answer for this. I am sure Ajit can answer, but now that he is constrained by immediate electoral politics he might not be in a position to give a clear reply. Perhaps what might be a verity in economics might well be a disaster in politics, if uttered publicly."

"Doesn't matter," Chakraborti replied. "I can give all the answers that you, the CCP or the people want. In fact, that is now my life's mission. Under the License Quota Permit Raj, whole masses have been reduced to exactly the statistical data points you mention. This continues to this day even after two decades of so-called liberalisation. Let me quote our own Prof.B.R.Shenoy, who, in my humble opinion, was the best economist India produced in the last century.

"A society is free, when its citizens and individuals are free in the sense of being *independent of the arbitrary will of another.*

"The economic affairs of a free society are controlled and directed by truly sovereign consumers. Individuals function pragmatically in the economic sphere. This control and direction of the economy is affected by the price-regulated market mechanism. Businessmen interpret these prices and turnover signals to produce and deliver goods and services.

"Investments for these activities are sourced from the capital markets, which are integral to the price-regulated market mechanism. This includes domestic as well as foreign investments. These investments are channelled to produce according to consumer preferences.

"In the modern world, irrespective of the ideological hue, whether free, socialist, or communist, production involves time. Thus the production process for both industry and agriculture has to commence in anticipation of, and in advance of, demand. The signals for such anticipatory production are generated by the forward markets – another integral component of the price regulated market mechanism. The forward market represents a fairly accurate mechanism for predicting demand and changing market situations.

"Operationally, the first link in the chain of consumer directed economic system is trade, which interprets and transmits consumer decisions to the producers. Suppose a community is cut off from the national mainstream. Production for the bigger national market would be replaced by production to meet the fewer needs of a smaller community. Producers unable to reap economies of scale would be forced to increase prices, which will further drive demand, already low in a small community, further down. It is easy to imagine such a community slipping into primitive ways and into dire poverty.

"The absence of barriers to internal and external trade is a precondition for the full and efficient functioning of a free society. Logic and experience have shown that this freedom will permit continued prosperity for the economy, the result of the use of capacity of its specialised talents through integration of the national economy with the world markets, the demand of which, unlike the demands of limited national markets, may not be easily satisfied.

"Second, the full and efficient functioning of a free society demands recognition of the institution of private property, not only in respect of a family house, durable consumer goods in it and a car, but also in respect of capital assets, the means of production. In a free society, because of the discipline of a most ruthless consumer, the management, on pain of survival, has to keep continual watch over cost, quality and turnover. This calls for perpetual flexibility of decisions. Consumer discipline operates, in the case of the larger corporations, through its impact on the stock market quotations for the scrips of corporations. It is just not practical to achieve the requisite decision flexibility under social ownership, that is, ownership of no one in particular, of the means of production. Experience has shown that, the magic of ownership is among the most powerful forces making for progress.

"The third pre-condition for the full success of the consumer directed economic system is economic freedom of the individual. These may be expressed in the following terms. The distribution of income of an individual between consumptions and saving; the choice of consumption and the power to direct entrepreneurs through a price regulated market mechanism, to import, or to fabricate at home the commodities of his choice; the distribution of his savings among the several alternatives; the choice of his or her occupation. The above four freedoms constitute fundamental economic freedoms of citizens.

"Under conditions of consumer sovereignty, businessmen would strive to reduce costs and improve quality to retain their customers. Through shifts of resources and technological progress, with consumer approval, high cost, low quality goods and services would be replaced on a continuous basis by high quality and low cost products. This will lift up production, incomes and the general level of living.

"The main advantage of a consumer oriented economy is the rapid expansion in employment. The expansion of employment at current or rising wage rates is not a function of investment or that of a step down in the technology of production. It is solely a function of the expansion of overall production. Unemployment is liquidated in direct correlation with the rapid expansion of the national product.'

"Under full consumer sovereignty, there is no need, or indeed room, for monopolies in production, distribution, imports and exports. Incomes of all individuals would correspond to wages, interest, rent and profits and their respective contribution to the national product. There would be no room for a windfall, hence no one would be able to appropriate another's earnings. There will be no social injustice. In contrast, socialist economic systems abound in monopolies, privileges and subsidies, bringing to a few privileged individuals and groups unmerited incomes, at the expense of the rest of the community.

"Further, income differences tend to decline as economic development progresses. This is not only due to absence of social injustice, but also due to the natural decline in interest, rent, and profits –the earnings of the economic elite. On the other hand, there is a natural increase in wages and salaries. As a free economy progresses, the proportion of wages and salaries to the GDP increases."

"All this is very well," Paresh said, pouring more beer into both glasses. "But what about inflation? It seems to be both high and persistent."

"Allow me to quote the good professor again," Chakraborti replied, savouring his drink. The weather was getting warmer. "Inflation is a severely monetary phenomenon. It is an act of the State. An expansion of money results when aggregate government expenditure exceeds its aggregate receipts both on revenue and capital accounts and the ensuing budget deficit is covered by resorting to the printing press or which is the same thing, by borrowing from the Reserve Bank of India. This expansion of money supply becomes inflationary when it pushes up money supply per physical unit of national product."

This conversation, helped to convince Paresh that the JA would still have a fighting chance. He resolved to study Shenoy's works to gain a better understanding of economics. He wanted to share what he had learned with his friends and acquaintances. He understood that a large number of people were bereft of sound economic knowledge, thanks to the one-sided education system that preferred to teach ideology instead of ideas. Mental cobwebs had to be cleaned and the power of rational thinking implanted amongst even educated people. No government, however large its majority, would be able to set an agenda for good governance when the public at large were ignorant of basic good economics.

Chapter XII

'A Textbook Fascist', the headline screamed. The headline, in big bold letters, caught Paresh's attention. 'Ajit Kumar is a fascist according to Nirmal Padamji', the report began.

'I am not saying this,' the report continued, quoting Padamji. 'This is the conclusion of the eminent sociologist Dr. Kekre, who interviewed Ajit a few months ago. If you want any further evidence, you only have to see the contempt Ajit has for the elders in his own party. Everyone is aware of his haughty and imperious ways. This is undoubtedly why the venerable BGP split – a split induced by the power hunger of Shri Ajit Kumar, may I add.

'This may sound a trifle hypocritical to some, since I, my family and the CCP, have always fought against the BGP. Yet, in a democracy, there is a need for an opposition party. To that extent, I regret the current travails that the BGP is undergoing because of one person's hunger for power.

'If you think that I am playing politics about this, I admit that you are right. Is it wrong to politicise an issue and to stop a person whose ascendancy can only mean the greatest danger to the very existence of our republic? A person who is the very antithesis of the qualities embedded in the Directive Principles of our Constitution? The very Constitution that has brought equality, dignity and progress for the millions, oppressed for the past so many centuries? The answer to that question is a thundering NO!'

Paresh put the paper away. He felt tired with the stale arguments put forth by Padamji. However, with such political sharp shooters like Padamji and obvious compradors in the mainstream press at work, how could Ajit ever make an impression on the electorate, let alone win it? If meaningful reforms had to be carried out, a working majority in the Lok Sabha was the first essential requirement. Would JA even get near it, even though they had boldly, if rashly, in Paresh's opinion, declared a target of winning 275 seats?

Almost as if in answer to Paresh's heartburn, Ajit convened a meeting of his close friends, dubbed the 'core committee' in the press. Ananthanarayan, a Tamil Brahmin was the convenor. He mainly discharged the duties of a secretary. An old associate, he was very loyal to Ajit and completely honest. He called Paresh and asked him to create an archive of the proceedings of the meeting online, accessible only to core committee members.

Aditya Patel had been a successful businessman before Ajit tapped him for a party post. Aditya had already made his millions, but it had not brought him recognition; there were plenty of other successful businessmen and women from Gujarat. So, when Ajit had invited him to join the BGP, he had jumped at the opportunity. Now, Jan Awaaz was his best chance to advance his political career. He was a good strategist and had a proven track record of winning elections for the BGP. Indeed, Lalwani had been insistent and desperate that he should stay back in the party, but the thought of striking out with a start-up outfit had sent his adrenaline racing. He decided to back Ajit, who had been instrumental in bringing him into politics.

Jayashree Mandal was a big name in the Uttar Pradesh wing of BGP. Her joining the JA was most unexpected, because she was connected most closely with identity politics from which Ajit had distanced himself. Her plump figure disguised a shrewd political brain and almost inexhaustible energy while on the campaign trail – qualities that Ajit valued greatly.

Jagdishwar Singh had a strong following in Rajasthan, but could not be trusted. He had never exhibited much interest in Ajit's work. He had been with the CCP and had hopped onto the BGP following differences with Padamji.

Surendranath was Ajit's commander in Bihar. His loyalty to Ajit was not in doubt, but his ability to carry the state was.

That left Aslam Ali Khan and John Varghese. Aslam was the Muslim face of BGP in UP and he was an asset to Ajit in countering Padamji's onslaughts on Ajit's secular credentials. Varghese, a media professional, had been prominent in Atmaji's movement. His contacts and talents would prove invaluable in the media war that would surely break out, now that elections were near. Ajit realised that winning the media battles were as important to the party's success as street level campaigning. In the mainstream media, Padamji held a clear advantage. Ajit had to wage an unconventional battle, a media guerrilla war, if he wanted to succeed. The frontline troops in these special operations were his legion of fans on the Internet. Ajit wanted to use them to rouse the large number of Net-savvy youth to vote for the JA. This was a classic indirect approach to achieve a goal.

The key person however was Jaideep Sanyal. An economist and psephologist by profession, he had undertaken extensive research into the electorate and knew each state's political landscape like the back of his hand.

An impressed Paresh had no doubt that this team and its strategy would succeed. He worked with redoubled vigour to network with his friends and associates towards this goal. His task of archiving meant that he had first-hand information of core committee meetings, as recorded by Ananthanarayan. The records were then studied by both Sanyal and Chakraborti, who fleshed out the minutes into meaningful reports. Paresh then archived them with appropriate cyber security measures.

Ajit planned to pick Sanyal's brains to formulate a strategy to counter and prevail over Padamji and the CCP. The meeting was held at Ajit's home and Paresh and Chakraborti were invited to attend. They could witness but not participate in the meeting. He reached Ajit's house well before the appointed time.

The walls were crowded with photos and memorabilia from Ajit's hockey playing days. There was a three-seater sofa on one side, backed up against a window. It faced a 26-inch LCD TV on a simple trolley. On the sofa's left were two single sofas that looked comfortable despite the well-worn covers. For the rest of the group, Sonal, Ajit's wife had brought up the dining chairs. Anantharaman was the first to arrive, a little before six, followed by Jayashree. The rest came in one by one, and all were assembled by ten minutes past six.

There was tea, samosas and biscuits and some hugely bruised egos in that room. Many in the group were still grappling with Ajit's dramatic decision and their expulsion from the party by Lalwani's group. Even though they had formally resigned, their hands had been forced by Lalwani. Now they had to show that Ajit enjoyed the support of the masses and that, in the forthcoming elections, they would not become history.

Paresh knew that Ajit's worry was different. He was really not bothered about winning. His concern was that the public mood had reached such a level of frustration that, if a new, dynamic and honest leadership did not emerge, the country could well plunge into chaos. Paresh saw that Ajit's attitude puzzled the rest.

"Friends," Ajit said, addressing the group, "thanks for being here and reposing confidence in me. Jaideep here has come up with some interesting ideas. Let's hear them first before we begin the discussions."

Jaideep cleared his throat. "As usual, Ajit is being kind. Many of the things I am going to speak about will clearly bear the imprimatur of his thought. All I have done is to collate the ideas, form a strategy and conduct research to test our hypotheses.

"First, the back ground. No doubt, there is a lot of angst in the nation today. People are tiring of the same old slogans put forward by the CCP, no less than the same old excuses for non-performance. Corruption is the real game changer. People seem prepared to go to great lengths, some would even admit to 'going to any lengths', to stamp down on corruption.

"This then is our first opportunity. People are ready for change. What it requires is an inspiring leader around which the opposition can coalesce." Everyone automatically turned to look at Ajit. "The threat, of course, is Padamji. He has age on his side, and, if he changes course even now, there is a good chance that the voting public will choose him. No doubt, the mainstream media would sing hosannas with glib slogans like 'Change with Continuity'. They would not be particularly bothered that, for change to be real and meaningful there should be discontinuity with past policies. The good news is that nobody takes Lalwani seriously." There was a collective exhalation amidst the group. "Yet, the threat is, however negligible it might be, that he could cut into our vote share. In a closely fought election, those few votes could mean the difference between victory and defeat. The difference between whether we have 300 plus seats or sink irremediably into single digits."

"Will such a small percentage of votes really mean that much?" Jayashree broke in. If Jaideep felt any resentment at being interrupted, he did not show it.

"Yes," he answered smoothly. "What with the first past the post system, even a few thousand votes spread over several constituencies can win us many seats. This approach relates to the heartland states, where the BGP has been traditionally strong. But, to penetrate other areas like Bengal, the South and the Northeast, Ajit and I have developed a new idea. I have tested this quietly and there seems to be a good chance that it would work. To overcome this difficulty with the regional leaderships, we propose what we call the 'subaltern strategy'.

"The main proposition of this strategy is that the leadership of regional states will be averse to linking up with us, as they are all a part of the Delhi Consensus – the incestuous network of crony capitalists, venal politicians and corrupt bureaucrats, comprador media and confrontational labour leaders, which has been the ruin of our country. Our problem is that we have to state clearly that we are dead against corruption. This means a new set of policies, a paradigm shift. Our new policies must be completely different from the current policies and laws, all of which have been enacted with an eye to extracting what economists euphemistically call 'rent'. In fact, Ajit has gone hammer and tongs against these tendencies in his public speeches. There is no need to add that all his speeches have been very well received by the public.

"Wherever I checked, I found that the second-rung leadership in many cases, and third and lower rung cases in almost all regional parties, are fed up with their respective leadership. These leaders are seen as lining their own pockets, with the lower level leadership, not to say anything about the cadres getting only 'trickle down benefits', if any. Ronald Reagan would undoubtedly turn over in his grave, if he learnt how our politicians have subverted his famed economic theory. Further, the lower-rung people, who are in closer contact with the public, are acutely aware of the sea change in public attitude towards corruption and inflation. I am sure that most of them will be only too happy to flee the sinking ships that these regional parties today represent. This, then, is the other major opportunity for us.

"Our proposal is to approach these dissatisfied elements in the parties and to offer a value proposition. Support us, and some amongst you will get tickets to Lok Sabha seats, some to assembly seats, while the majority would be given public recognition. The most important, of course, would be that, in choosing to support Ajit, they would be backing the winning horse for whom the youth of the country cherish a strong admiration. This could well translate into support for years to come.

"Another finding is that almost all of them either admire or are well disposed towards Ajit. Thus, this is a gambit that could work, and with big results. We could even envisage a two-thirds majority if we get this right."

"It sounds good, but can we make it happen? I mean, others would also react if we started poaching from their stables." Jayshree had a point there.

"I don't propose to take any Tom, Dick, or Harry who wants to tag along," Ajit spoke up. "We know that there are some people who gel with us on ideological issues – we will target only such people. Most probably the parties and the leaders will wish these guys good riddance. In most cases, the lower rung leaders pose a threat to the dynastic leadership. You know, even regional parties are now mostly dynastic.

"Further, I would also like to mention the communication strategy," Ajit continued earnestly. "Just as there will be overt messaging, we need to implement below-the-line messaging as well. We must have people approaching households independently to reinforce our main message. In addition, we already have networks like Teach India to Read. Of course, I had promised that I would not make political use of such organisations and I won't. But a big group of people who actively participated in that program are now supporting JA. We can use this support as a social force multiplier."

"I think the circle will be completed when we negotiate seat sharing with regional parties." Aditya Patel was already working on a poll strategy. "They may not want a pre-poll alliance. What we should do is to negotiate seat-sharing arrangements with them as quietly as possible, even surreptitiously – and even with the subaltern elements Sanyal mentioned. This will certainly maximise the number of seats we win. For the regional outfits as well, this would be a winning strategy as the CCP is their number one opponent in a number states. I think they would like to maximise their victories at the cost of the CCP."

"Excellent idea," Ajit beamed. "Hope all of you think over the matters we have spoken about today and develop detailed plans that can be implemented by the cadre. Ananth, send out a summary of this meeting to the group. Our campaign will now revolve around these ideas. Any new ideas you all bring up are welcome – they can be added to this list. This list will form the core strategy for the elections."

Chapter XIII

"The proposed reforms the JA has put out seems to be very radical. Can you elaborate on the background for all this? Why you think such drastic changes are necessary?" Kiran Butt was interviewing Ajit. For this interview, Divya had made extensive preparations under Kiran's directions. She gave her a bunch of questions to ask, but Kiran ignored those during the actual interview. She simply went on asking the usual questions.

"Overall, the administration would emphasise transparency and fairness, and ease of dealing with government departments, "Ajit looked at Kiran." The aim of all these reforms is to unleash the latent potentiality of the people as also to ensure that local and national monopolies do not grab all the opportunities.

"Previously, and even at present, when one approaches a government, nothing seems to move. Not only would you have to know who to contact, you would also have to satisfy that person. I am sure you know what I mean. Today, we have the situation of a round robin economy. This is still essentially the 'know who' model, except that everyone apparently knows 'who' that one particular person is. But then, that 'known' person directs you to another, who directs you to yet another and so on. Even the name round robin is imperfect, for, at the end of the cycle, you will not end up with the first person you met, but the ultimate person.

"These are the sort of shenanigans that we want to do away with if we form the government."

"On the welfare front as well, you have made suggestions that many say are impractical."

"Any effort at reform is bound to run into rough weather. The reason is not that people do not want to change; the reason is the fear of the unknown. The fear of whether the new system will work as promised. It is for this very reason that we have said that, while we will implement reforms in stages, the objective would be announced loudly and clearly right at the beginning. People can very well judge for themselves if the component parts of the policy lead towards the stated goals. This should allay most if not all such fears and consequent resistance to change.

"Apart from government efforts, which will continue, private companies and NGOs would be allowed to perform welfare delivery. This would be monitored and properly audited. Local representatives would also be appointed to take care of local issues."

"How will you deal with public sector enterprises and the huge losses they have run-up?"

"I think it was Rajaji who said that every time a public enterprise raises its price it is a concealed tax. I believe that in the present context, we would have to continue with public enterprises since the lives of so many people are intimately intertwined with the fortunes of these companies. However, we will expect them to perform well financially. You must understand that the number of consumers served by these companies is much larger than the number employed in those enterprises. Here is a classic case of Mancur Olson's theory at work. The much larger number of consumers are practically held to ransom by the numerically smaller number of employees. Don't get me wrong. I am not saying that employees' welfare should be ignored. Just that it is intimately connected to and best assured, when we keep the consumers interest in mind while making policy.

"Public sector companies would be grouped under three or more holding companies. The present system of different ministries managing various enterprises would be done away with. This is a hangover from the Stalinist past. Job reservations would continue by special legislation. We will implement management reforms to cut losses. Where necessary, we will induce mergers and acquisitions, so that companies perform organically and profitably. Sales of shares of public enterprises would accrue to a special capital fund. The profits of these enterprises would also go to this fund. This can be used to fund further capital expenses or be transferred to the National Social Welfare Fund."

"Thank you Shri Ajit Kumar for your exposition of your party's policies. I wish you the best of luck in the elections."

At that moment, Divya realised that Kiran was playing to Padamji's script.

"Welcome to the Face-off program. Our guest today is the President of the CCP, Mr. Padamji." The camera panned to show Padamji, whose face was lit up by a genial smile. The camera stayed for a moment on Padamji, then rose slowly, still keeping his smiling face in focus, as the shot dissolved. Divya was impressed. This was one of the techniques used in movies to earn the hero sympathy of the audiences.

Padamji was dressed in a white pajama and kurta. For the interview, he had added a light brown Nehru jacket that emphasised his broad shoulders. He looked svelte and handsome. Divya held her breath, waiting for Rai to ask his first question. She had agreed with Paresh that they should watch the program and share their views on Whatsapp.

"Before I start my questions," Tony Rai said, "I would like to congratulate you on your stand on pro-poor policies. I am sure you would have received much praise for that." Padamji nodded, his face still holding that genial smile from the previous shot.

Paresh wondered how long it was humanly possible for a man to keep that expression.

"You have always championed the cause of the poor and down trodden, yet, now, you face a situation where you are accused of continuing a political dynasty. In the context of the upcoming elections, how do you plan to handle this?"

Padamji permitted himself a short laugh; less charitable viewers like Paresh felt that it resembled a hyena's.

"Let me make it plain at the outset," Padamji began in his stylish Oxbridge accent. "I am not at all worried with such juvenile charges. I am what I am. I cannot help my birth; I have some advantages and many disadvantages with such a birth. Can I help it if my parents and their parents have been in politics? No. I think the only reason these people are cribbing is that my parents and grandparents were successful in what they did. They were true nationalists, and they achieved a lot for the country. I sincerely feel that jealousy against their great achievements is at the bottom of such charges."

'Yeah', Paresh typed, 'you can't change your birth, but you CAN change your profession!'

"You say that we should spread sweetness and sunshine around, and that everyone should partake of the benefits of growth and not just the froth at the top of the cup."

"Yes," Padamji was emphatic. "Our policy through the decades has been to give the poor and downtrodden a helping hand. We do not care much for the so-called industrialists. Crony capitalists all." Here Padamji made a gesture belittling these cronies, bringing his thumb and fingers together and throwing them out. "No doubt it is because my family has been steadfast in upholding the interests of the poor that my family and I are damned for being dynasts."

'That is a nice touch', wrote Divya, who was watching the programme from the comfort of her home. 'This is a good shot at earning sympathy.'

"The JA seems to be campaigning on a completely different note. How do you plan to take them on?"

"The JA's policies are rotten. It smacks of an earlier brutal era of zamindars, robber barons and crony capitalists. In fact, it seems to be their policy to resurrect and support this archaic and destructive force – unlike the CCP, which stands proudly at the vanguard of the people's movement. We are cut from a different cloth. We respect women's rights, and the rights of minorities. We respect freedom of expression. We want free flow of information. That is why

I insisted that government should pass an act of securing information rights to the people.

"I am sure that JA does not like any of this, though, for purposes of political survival, they genuflect to these progressive ideas and values. At the core, deep inside every person, there resides the beast of greed. JA's sole intention seems to be to unleash this beast on an ignorant public. We know this beast cannot be eliminated. Hence, we devise controls and procedures to contain this beast. Ours is an agenda for the future prosperity of every citizen, while maintaining harmony with the environment."

'My blood boils when I hear these inanities delivered so smoothly', Paresh wrote. 'I think that Rai is asking questions that would set off CCP's programs, while trashing JA's policies. How frustrating! How can anyone, least of all an ordinary citizen like me, protest against such blatant abuse by the press?'

'This is normal, some channels do this for Ajit too', Divya replied.

'Name one', came the furious rejoinder. 'Maybe, if enough numbers protested, then the cry of press freedom in danger and fascism would fill the air. And from the very crowd that was using its power positions to advance its own interests, be it in economics, politics, history, diplomacy or even in science. Yes even the hard sciences too were used selectively', Paresh recalled.

'How so?'

'When the story of Ganesha drinking milk broke, the CSIR rushed to declare it a scientific phenomenon only.'

'Oh that.'

Paresh sighed as he signed off. There was only so much he could do. If he could not convince Divya, what chance did he have of convincing the rest of the world? He just hoped that the little he was doing for JA would be enough to uproot the likes of Padamji.

Belatedly, Divya remembered her promise to Paresh, and, seeking to make amends, she called Paresh. She intended to make some polite conversation before coming to the topic of Ranjan and Padamji. But it was only after about 10 minutes that Divya was able to recollect the reason for her call.

"I think Ranjan did have a deal with Padamji. Maybe not now, but certainly back then at the height of the anti-corruption movement. But I have not been able to pin down anything yet."

"Yeah…thanks," Paresh replied. "I thought as much. Anyway, all that is in the past. In a sense the future is upon us as the elections draw nearer and nearer. I hope the people of India realise where their true interests lie and vote for JA."

"I agree," Divya forced herself to reply. "I too would like a change, but Padamji is not all that bad as he is being made out to be. Trust me. I have met him in person and he is very charming."

"What?" She could feel the surprise and outrage in Paresh's voice. She felt distressed. She now had the strange feeling that any friend of hers must be acceptable to Paresh.

She was surprised at the animosity Padamji's name evoked in Paresh. She knew that Padamji was not fully sincere, but then again, which politician was? She did not agree with many of his policies, much less his politics. Yet, the slick way in which he presented himself to the world and the way the media, even a stalwart like Tony Rai, bent over backwards to accommodate him, impressed her. He had power and he knew how to use it.

How would Ajit and his ideology measure up to against such an excellent exponent of politics? Was idealism even relevant in the present age? These questions bothered Divya. She felt a need to express herself, but she was wary of communicating such thoughts to friends in the media. There was always a chance that it would get around, and she might be put in an embarrassing situation. She called Paresh again. "Can we meet somewhere? I want to talk about what we were discussing just now."

"Sure." Paresh sounded enthusiastic. "There is a little place around the corner from our office. We can talk there... the tea and especially the samosas are good." Divya agreed readily.

"Say it's like this," she said when they were comfortably seated across a small table. He seemed a little taken aback at first at the subject she had chosen.

"I hope you don't mind..." Divya eyed him anxiously.

"No...not at all. I will answer you from what I have learnt from Chakraborti and from Ajit's site. One must be a realist to survive in this world. Indeed, all true idealists realise this. An ideal is an objective, a state that gives the most satisfaction in physical and psychological terms. To achieve this would require practical steps. Even, collectivists like Lenin, Stalin and Mao understood this. Thus, in the first years of the Soviet Union, a free market existed along with state controls. It was Stalin who moved to the next level of control. Communism is an ideal, a state of being that many wish to achieve. Yet, in obtaining this state of nirvana, horrendous violence was perpetrated. In the Soviet Union, millions of peasants were massacred to achieve collectivisation of land, while millions more perished in the Great Leap forward under Mao.

"I like the concept of liberty, precisely because it seeks change through consensus and not through force. Consensus can be amongst a group, a region, an entire nation, or just between two individuals. When two individuals enter into a contract voluntarily, without force being used on either side, a revolution has occurred. A free society is built upon thousands of such contracts. Thus, change occurs 'naturally' as a reaction to an emerging situation. Now, you might legitimately ask if things will occur only in reaction to some other event. I know the 'reactionary' theory of the communists – that is not what I am referring to. Is it not true that every person reacts almost on a daily basis, to his or her environment, colleagues, and developments at the workplace? Thus, when someone 'reacts' to a given situation such as poverty and discovers a new contraption, a new way of marketing or a new way of organisation, then we have what social scientists call 'progress'. You must always remember that social sciences are inexact, unlike the 'hard' sciences like physics or chemistry. Thus, in social science, there is obviously a chance for a person's environment and his view of the world, encapsulated in the German term 'weltchaunwang' to play a part.

"It was in reaction to his burning desire for personal recognition and to end his poverty that Alexander Graham Bell invented the telephone, and Edison the electric lamp. It is always 'reaction' to a given situation that motivates human action."

Divya would have loved to know and hear about Paresh's 'reactions' to her. Prudence dictated that she refrain from expressing herself.

"Padamji repeatedly claims that Ajit is dictatorial; this is rich. In his own party is there anyone who can stand up to him? Anyway who can dare to say that he is authoritarian?"

"No one," acknowledged Divya. "Yet, today, he is the centre of power in India. It would not be wise to ignore that either."

"Divya, are you saying that we should not aspire to the ideals we share?" She sensed that Paresh, felt uncomfortable with her present take on Padamji.

"No, just that it would be wise to be practical. I mean if you want a job, you try to impress the interviewer. There is no need for you to like him or her, is there?"

Paresh was obviously not happy with this. "I agree with you on this. Yet, I feel distinctly uncomfortable when we make compromises of this sort. Is this why so many people are falling over themselves to ingratiate themselves with Padamji? What magic does he wield that even hardened journalists and professionals are so gung-ho about him?"

Divya could assure Paresh on this question. "Simple," she said. "It is the herd mentality. When celebs like Tony Rai and Kiran fawn on him, others follow suit. For many people, particularly the self-professed 'liberals', a certificate of good conduct from these two seems to be enough for their purposes. Moreover you get these columnists and hardly successful authors certifying him as charming, liberal and well... everything noble, just after a single meeting with him. Do I need to say anything more?"

"What we need, to get us out this situation, is a superman." His heavy sigh made his feelings plain. He leaned forward; her tobacco perfume teased his nostrils."We need a man of ideas as well as a man of action. Someone, who knows the answers, and has the ability to implement them, somebody with proven administrative skills. Someone, who would take the side of the common people and not that of the vested interests."

"Who should not take the side of the vested interests?" Chakraborti stood over them with a genial smile. Paresh repeated what he had said, pushing his chair back.

"Ajit," Chakraborti said firmly. "Ajit is all that and more." For some reason he could not understand, his audience did not seem to share his enthusiasm.

Chapter XIV

The Election Commission announced the poll schedule. Pollsters and journalists predicted a hung Parliament in the three-way competition. Ajit's first interview at the beginning of the polling season was with Tony Rai. Ajit wanted Paresh to report on how the interview would look to an ordinary viewer. Paresh would watch the interview and make notes on a list of items identified by Ajit's media team. There would be others, like Paresh who would carry out this task. Ajit considered it important to gauge the impact he was making on the electorate.

Tony Rai began: "I have pleasure in interviewing you, particularly as it is the first of any party leader since the elections were announced two days ago."

Ajit replied, "Thank you."His tone was mechanical. Paresh settled down in the sofa, trying to take in every word that was spoken.

"Pollsters say that the most likely result would be a hung parliament. Have you sometimes thought that you made a mistake in quitting the BGP? Our figures show that with you in, they might have just swung it."

"I think that I have already answered this question several times and adequately at that. However, I will answer again. The reason I quit is not political at all in the sense of gaining an electoral advantage or anything like it. It was born out of conviction – the conviction that, for the nation to pull itself out of poverty, things must change and radically. The people in the BGP were not ready for such a complete change, even though there was widespread public support for such a programme. Not that the BGP is a bad party –just that it has become moribund and somehow more and more like the CCP they seek to replace. The reason I quit was to try and bring about that change. If people respond and vote us to power in the coming elections that would give us an opportunity to serve the nation." Ajit shrugged. "But if they choose caution, so be it. We would be happy to sit in the opposition. What will not stop is our outreach to the public, to educate them on the changes needed and how to bring them about. Personally, if, tomorrow, the BGP or the CCP for that matter embraces our position then I will be the first person to support them. I am not here seeking the office of PM. I want the office of PM only in order to bring about change. If somebody else can do that, I have no problem in supporting them."

"That is a very risky statement to make, for a politician."

Ajit merely smiled, not bothering to answer, despite Rai giving him more than a minute to reply. Paresh punched his fist in the air. This was the way to go. Give Rai a taste of his own medicine.

Rai recovered ground by changing the subject.

"The JA does not have much of a presence in several states – one of them is Kerala. This state is highly literate and the people are sophisticated. It offers a fascinating if complex political picture. What are your plans to crack this state?"

"You are right. Kerala is all that you said, and the people are indeed very politicised. I consider this to be the bane of the state, though your question seems to imply that that is its strength. A high level of politicisation implies that people act collectively."

Tony nodded albeit reluctantly, as if agreeing with Ajit would in some way taint him. "The people of Kerala certainly score high on politics. However, in economic terms, where is the state? They are a hard working, smart people. The state's prosperity is largely generated from across the Arabian Sea in the Gulf countries and from other states in India. There is hardly any industrial employment in Kerala, though they are doing well in the tourism sector. For me, industrial jobs per se are not 'superior' to other walks of life. What is important is that each region and people should do what comes best to them.

"My idea is that people should put economics first. This means that they should act individually. This logic is quite plain. If you want a job, you have to go and get it. If you want to start an industry, then the individual has to do something that sets the ball rolling. Tourism is also an industry and, if nurtured properly, could become a game-changer for Kerala, in terms of employment. Thus, individual action wins out over collective action as far as economics is concerned." Ajit paused to take a sip of water.

"Despite their sophistication and other noteworthy achievements, I feel that Kerala will come into its own, as and when it prioritises economics over politics. Then, its people would truly benefit from the bounty of natural beauty that nature has thought fit to shower on Kerala."

"There is an opinion, shared by many, that your leadership style is dictatorial. Your reaction?"

"I have a certain viewpoint and I stick to it until I see that I am wrong. Is this dictatorial? For example, I don't believe in allowing anyone to be corrupt or indulge in corrupt practises. So I try to be strict and monitor bureaucrats and ministers closely. Simply because they can't 'seek rent', if they claim they are being stifled and I am authoritarian, then so be it."

"You speak so much about the private sector, and you also have this image of being pro-business – but the defining moment for capitalism came in 2008 in the U.S., when banks failed and the government had to step in to bail them out. The reason for the market failure was ascribed to the greed of bankers and businessmen. Padamji has specifically charged you with…" Rai consulted his notes, "Quote, 'The beast of greed. JA's sole intention seems to be to unleash this beast on to an ignorant public'. Unquote."

"I want to know if greed will not affect the men and women once they take employment in government and look forward to retiring on a healthy pension? Is it Shri Padamji's case that only ordinary people, the vast majority of the people of our country who work outside government alone are subject to greed? Or is it his case that only the people outside government are capable of human emotions, those in government being super human?

"The problem in 2008 was not market failure, as you put it. At its back was the availability of easy credit at low interest rates for a much longer period than any market could afford.

That could happen only if there was interference from the government – and there was. The U.S. Federal Reserve did keep interest rates very low for a very long time. Hence, it ought to have come as no surprise that businessmen overextended themselves. The logical way to have dealt with that crisis would have been to allow the banks to fail."

"Wouldn't the depositors have lost money for no fault of theirs?"

"Firstly, the main complaint was that banks, far from nurturing depositors, actually lent monies borrowed from other financial institutions in the market. This was the crux of the crisis. Once a certain section of the securitised debt became bad, people were afraid to lend even against good securities. This jammed up the banking system. Yes, I know it sounds harsh, but unless we allow failure, we cannot build success. We would not get the prudent, the honest, and the good entrepreneurs to run innovative businesses. Yes, for depositors to lose money would have been bad. The government could simply have paid them off. It would have probably cost less and would have taught bad bankers a good lesson. The way things actually panned out, the bad guys won. Moral hazards were ignored and everybody had their debts backed up, whether or not they had exercised due diligence and prudence in their business dealings, be it borrowing or lending.

"About your other point about being pro-business, I believe that the government must facilitate business. However, I also believe that this should not be done on a selective, case-by-case basis. This leads to crony capitalism. More than being pro-business, I am for free markets, which is a system. In this system, everybody is equal. There can be no room for monopolies or cronyism. The poor and disadvantaged can also aspire to become big businessmen, or make a satisfactory living without depending on public money or private charity."

"Still on economics, you say that policies will take some time to yield results. But Lord Keynes said that in the long run we are all dead, implying that measures should work fast. He also called for robust intervention from the government to tackle economic cycles and to promote development. Your comments." From the smug expression on his aristocratic face, Rai clearly felt that this question would floor Ajit.

"Measures that we take should begin working fast, but, as Peter Drucker pointed out, we will be able to rid ourselves of poverty only at the end of the development cycle. I only ask that policies should be consistently followed for this duration. Sir John Cowperthwaite, the late Financial Secretary of Hong Kong, said, 'In the long run, the aggregate of decisions of individual businessmen, exercising individual judgment in a free economy, even if often mistaken, is less likely to do harm than the centralised decisions of a government, and certainly the harm is likely to be counteracted faster'.

"Similarly the government can do a lot in helping to develop infrastructure, basic education and such. Where interventionists go wrong is when they try to play God, in the form of Planning Commissions, the 'I know best' attitude, and in trying to second-guess consumer needs and what is even worse, new and emerging technologies."

"Turning to social harmony, there are people who say that you are actually a communalist, and that behind your goody-goody front you harbour fundamentalist feelings.

Or, at least, that fundamentalist forces would be unleashed under your regime."

"The sort of secularism practised in India now is twisted. Secularism is a political principle. In the West, this is taken to mean that there is a separation between the Church or religious orders and the State. In India this ought to mean that whatever your religion, that will not matter to the State. It should treat everyone equally. In the hands of the ruling clique, this principle has been turned upside down, to mean vote bank politics. This is not about just one party – many, if not most, parties are guilty. Their argument is that some persons and groups are more equal than others. Otherwise, what is the necessity for so many 'concessions' or 'benefits'? As pointed out repeatedly, these concessions hardly benefit and the so-called minorities still languish in ignorance and poverty.

"The other great error is to project a political principle onto private lives. Here, the guilt lies with the free 'liberal' intelligentsia. They say that one must practise the tokens of all religions to be really secular. They say I must not refuse to wear the insignia of particular faiths. Oh, really?

"In truth, while different people practise different religious rites, one practises what one believes in; and allows others to practise that which each may believe in. That is true secularism."

Chapter XV

Jai Singh, who led a caste-based party and had great influence among famers in the Hindi belt, announced that he would be joining Padamji's CCP in a pre-poll alliance. It would be called the Union for Common People. This would certainly diminish JA's chances in the crucial Gangetic belt. Paresh's stomach was in knots. Previously, it was thought that JA would get between 100 and 120 seats in the 170 odd seats in contestation in the region. 'The alliance would possibly mar JA's chances of victory in about half of those seats,' the TV blared. Angry and dispirited, Paresh switched off the TV. His nature was to take negatives in his stride – like the time he had narrowly flunked his preparatory tests for the CAT exam. In fact, the setback had energised him and he had worked hard and come out in flying colours in the actual exam, making it to IIM, Ahmedabad, which always had been his goal.

Now, he felt emptiness inside. He realised he had no fight left in him. Everyone seemed to find some fault or other with Ajit and many others like Jai Singh were joining Padamji. Paresh did not have a good opinion about Jai Singh. But he had hoped, fervently, that he would join Ajit in unseating the CCP. In fact, over these last few years, Jai had been raising his voice against the policies and scams of the CCP. Paresh found it very strange that he had now joined Padamji. He would have been happy if Jai had remained neutral – that way, JA would have scored well. If Singh had allied himself to JA, they would have swept North India and brought the coalition within striking distance of a simple majority.

Paresh reached for his mobile. He wanted to call Divya. She seemed to have answers to most of his questions on politics and she always managed to allay his doubts about JA's chances. A new and disturbing thought took root. Was he calling her because she was able to offer solace for his tensions induced by politics, or was it more particular and personal? He hurriedly sought to banish this subversive thought. Like water bubbling up in a fountain, this thought rose to the top of his mind every time he tried to push it down. Paresh shook himself, hoping to rid himself of the thought, but to no avail. The thought not only persisted but grew louder in volume. Then a new one came along. 'My dear Paresh', it said, 'are you about to make a fool of yourself?'

He shook his head vigorously in answer, and, catching himself in the act of doing so, felt even more disconcerted. New and strange sensations were coursing through him while his mind seemed to have taken a life of its own. Like a hot air balloon freed from its ropes, the mind wafted from place to place.

He finally gave up the chase and allowed his mind to paint a cosy picture of the future for him. There was Divya in it for sure. There were also a crowd of young boys and girls, whom Paresh did not know and did not want to know.

He saw a comfortable sofa, a pretty head on his lap, and a cascade of black hair pouring on to the floor.

Understandably, his voice was husky when he made the call to Divya. They spoke about many things and finally each convinced the other that it would be in their best interest to continue their volunteer work for JA. Paresh's good feelings did not last long. A couple of days later, the TV shows were full of a scandal. According to them, the JA had received overseas funding from doubtful sources, most probably the CIA. Paresh's sense of hopelessness increased when an anchor asked for the CCP's view about the 'whole affair'.

"It is pretty clear that the JA is funded by foreign organisations to destabilise the country and to impose neo colonial policies on it," the spokesperson declared with unholy glee. Paresh realised that the 'whole affair' was indeed of CCP's making. How to fight it was the question, especially when practically the entire mainstream media was parroting the CCP line? He racked his brains for a solution, but there was none.

He sighed. It was that riddle again. What to do when one did not have the faintest idea of what to do?

He had a bad night, with recurrent nightmares of Ajit and the JA being disqualified by the Election Commission. The saving grace was that each time he was consoled by Divya, who for some reason he could not understand, was always dressed in a wedding sari.

The morrow brought a good idea though. After consulting Ajit, Paresh and his colleagues launched an online campaign through social media. They gave whatever details they had, promising that more would be made available as and when the information became available. By afternoon they had cause to rejoice. The TV news bulletins carried a fifth headline stating that the JA had refuted the allegations of foreign funding. These were actually funds sent by party members residing overseas. All that had happened was that the funds had been collected by one person and remitted to India. Paresh was astonished how the anchors who had been shouting from the rooftops just the previous evening simply dropped the story as if nothing important had happened in between.

The episode taught Paresh and the whole party an important lesson; the power of the social media. When properly harnessed, it forced even the mightiest mainstream channel to change their stories. Paresh felt exultant. No longer would the media be able to blackmail the JA, with character assassination, selective leaks and false charges. The media would get an explosive reply if they resorted to these underhand means.

Chapter XVI

The big battle, the final poll duel, began with a CCP meeting in Mumbai. Padamji spoke to an impressively large crowd.

"It was here in 1942 that the clarion call for swaraj was given by Gandhiji. The CCP has specifically begun this campaign from Mumbai to mark this hallowed event." Padamji roared. "Even now, we are engaged in a freedom struggle – to free ourselves from the bondage of a neo-colonial world order, imposed on us by the rich countries and their friends here in India." Patel, standing behind and to one side of Padamji, raised his hand. Several members in the audience started clapping on cue. Padamji paused for the applause to subside. "My grandmother used to work 16 hours every day as Prime Minister. That means she dedicated two-thirds of her life to the welfare of this nation.

"I am not after power. My late parents taught me that power is a burden. My aim is to be a humble servant. There is a saying that power corrupts and absolute power corrupts absolutely. I do not want the corruptions of power." Then he raised his voice for the punch line. "If I get corrupted, who will you all have to turn to? So, I have decided not to assume power." Again, Patel's hand went up and again there was thunderous applause. "I have decided to sacrifice power, for the welfare of the nation." Deafening applause followed.

Anyone could have pointed out to Padamji the inherent contradictions in his statement. If power really corrupted and ought to be avoided, then how was it a 'sacrifice' to do so? Divya, who was watching the event in her office, laughed to herself. Hey, scriptwriter, get your act right! But how was it that Padamji had missed it? This questioned both intrigued and troubled Divya.

"We have taken several green initiatives. One programme is for solar energy – we have announced a 50% subsidy on putting up solar power plants. We have also levied tariffs on import of solar equipment – this will promote local manufacture. Further, the new Centre for Development of Alternative Energy, C-DAE, will focus on indigenous development of solar, windmill and other green technologies to produce electric power. I am sure that in few years we will be able to avoid technology imports along with their high costs from the developed countries.

"We have also passed laws making it mandatory for corporates to fund schooling, hospitals and so on around their factories. By passing this law, we have forced them to care for welfare of the people and not look only for profit. 'Put people before profits', that is our motto." Again, Patel raised his hand and there was a loud round of applause.

Divya was struck by this statement. From what she had learned from Paresh and Chakraborti, this particular initiative would considerably blunt Indian businesses' ability to remain competitive on the world stage. No other country had such laws. Thus, instead of doing business and serving their customers, Indian businesses would be forced to expend their energies in work for which the government or other social organisations were best suited.

"I pledge that I will solve the problems that face us today, such as unemployment, poverty and inflation, in a straight forward manner. After all, these problems affect the entire society and we must work towards a collective response, particularly for the eradication of poverty. Unless there is equity in the distribution of income, there can be no eradication of poverty. Even if there is only one chapatti left, I say that all of us must share it equally." This time, the crowd applauded wildly even though Patel's hand was firmly by his side.

"The CCP has decided to dedicate itself to the common people of India. We will work for your welfare. Our aim is to tax the rich people and distribute it to the poor. We will introduce more welfare measures if we are elected." Patel's hand did its work and Padamji had to wait for the applause to subside."You will be aware of all the welfare schemes we have already introduced, like food assurance, life insurance for all, rights to women, equitable compensation for land acquisition and free medicines. All these are yours and will be yours forever if you elect the CCP." This time, there was no need for Patel to raise his hand. The cheers were spontaneous; the crowd was learning fast.

"The question is, are you the people getting all these benefits? Is the bureaucracy actually transferring these goodies to the common folk? Do you have problems in accessing these schemes? The answer seems to be 'yes', unfortunately.

"Many people come and complain to me that when they go to government offices with some grievance, the officials do not hear them. Worse still, the officials act arrogantly and even demand illegal gratification. As a step to ensure the due rights of the populace particularly that of the illiterate masses in the countryside, I propose to enact a Right to Be Heard Act."Patel's hand did its work and a loud round of applause ensued. "When this act is passed everyone will be able to go to any government office and their voices, hitherto suppressed for thousands of years will be heard."

Padamji beamed at the audience. Divya knew that he was doing this for the benefit of the TV cameras. Due to security considerations, the audience were placed about a hundred feet from him and certainly would not be able to make out his facial features clearly.

Padamji categorically stated that he would nationalise practically everything so that the 'poor' could benefit. With 'profit' eliminated, he claimed, prices too would drop. Yet there was one statement of Padamji's that she found strange. She was sure that no economist would endorse him when Padamji claimed that PSU's (Public Sector Units) should make losses to benefit the people.

She was wrong – when reactions were invited from several economists, some of them hedged, while quite a few of them not only welcomed his statements but said that the implementation of such an revolutionary idea heralded the dawn of a new era of prosperity, equity, and welfare for the nation.

Divya was blown away by Padamji's charm and graciousness as an individual. Yet, she was aware that Padamji's economic ideas were detrimental to the nation.

A bewildered Divya called up Paresh. He seemed to know a lot about these things even though he was only a techie and not an economist. Paresh's number was busy. She tried again, with the same result. Who was he talking to for such a long time? Was it a girl she wondered, with an involuntary shudder. She badly wanted to know who Paresh was talking to. She knew that she would be very upset to learn that it was some other girl.

"Who were you talking to? Been trying for half an hour." She challenged him when he returned her call. There was a moment of silence. To Divya it seemed to last forever.

"Uhh...a call from office."

"Even when you are on leave?" Divya's suspicion was perfectly clear from her tone.

"See...they want to send me overseas." Paresh sounded dull. Divya exhaled; she wanted to shout with delight.

Very much relieved, she said, "Is that all?"

"What do you mean, is that all? I don't want to go."

"Because of the elections?"

"No!" The vehemence of Paresh's reply did funny things to her heart. "Anyway, it will be after the elections. But not very long afterwards from the looks of it."

"Oh." A thick clammy cold descended on Divya. Would she meet him again if he were to go away?

"How long?" She asked in a small voice.

"What? Oh...I expect to be away for about six months." Divya began to feel better. "Can't you postpone it or something?"

"It's just as you said. If I don't go, my next performance review would be hit for a six."

Divya could not trust herself to speak. She paused, trying to collect herself. She now asked the questions that had been uppermost in her mind just a little while ago on economics, even as they seemed totally irrelevant now. She hoped to subdue her tumultuous feelings by discussing such mundane subjects.

Paresh was forthright. "Many of these ideas were tried in the Soviet Union and the only thing that 'dropped' was the state itself. Unable to reconcile the contradictions of flawed economics, the country collapsed. This brings to light an important mistake that collectivists make. This is the economic calculation problem – the fallacy of controlled prices. Since the Soviets had no price mechanism, there was no way to know what each service or product actually cost. With certain given resources, how did one decide whether to build a house or a commercial establishment? This anomaly was brought out long ago by Ludwig Von Mises, the father of the Austrian school of economics. The famous challenge of Mises was uncompromising and to the point: 'Where there is no free market, there is no pricing mechanism: without a pricing mechanism, there is no economic calculation'."

"But Padamji says that with proper planning, with all the statistical data and tools at hand, all factors can be suitably addressed and accounted for."

"Look, it was von Hayek, who said that the major problem for the socialist planning board is its lack of knowledge. Without a market, the socialist planning board has no means of knowing the value-scales of the consumers, or the supply of resources, or available technologies. The capitalist economy is, for Hayek, a valuable means of disseminating knowledge from one individual to another through the pricing signals of the free market.

"According to Mises, the central problem is not knowledge. He clearly says that even if the socialist planners knew perfectly the value priorities of the consumers and wanted to satisfy them, and even if they enjoyed a perfect knowledge of all resources and all technologies, they still would not be able to calculate, for lack of a price system, of the means of production to be employed."

"But prices can be calculated with reference to costs. You can then add the nominal and reasonable profit to arrive at the correct value of a product." Paresh knew by now that Divya was not alone in making this argument. His sessions with Chakraborti had not only cleared his misconceptions, he was now a master in the subject.

"Right. This is what many people believe and maybe it is taught in many colleges. The truth is this; price is an intensely subjective matter. For example, on a dark night, with a whiff of rain in the air, you flag down an auto. Your home is two kilometres away and the fare costs Rs. 25 normally. On that day though it is still only eight o'clock, the driver demands Rs. 40. I am sure most people would agree to pay. You may call this exploitation. But the reason for the price is simple. At that moment, the demand for a mode transport is one. As it happens the supply is also one. You may refuse and wait for another, but you don't know whether it will start raining, or, even if another auto does come along that that would be unoccupied. You have a choice. Accept the terms or reject. Remember, the driver has not used force to have his way. He simply has made an offer and it is up to you to accept or reject. This is where the subjectivity part comes in. It is your desire to be safely home before rain starts that impels your decision. At this point in time, the costs of the trip, the auto driver's earnings from that trip are all essentially irrelevant. What counts is your need and want, and here he is eagerly waiting to fulfil it, albeit at a cost. You can try bargaining. If he accepts a lesser price, it reflects your capability to negotiate. Yet at the moment your capacity to bargain is weak and his is strong. So if you want that trip you take his price, voluntarily. I hope you are now clear on how prices 'signal' markets. When there is demand, as prices rise, it tells businessmen that that product or service can be sold at that particular location and at a particular price. Accordingly they adjust their production schedules."

Chapter XVII

"I have come here to address you today as the President of the Jan Awaaz Party." Ajit was addressing a large crowd in Hyderabad. "I consider myself to be only a worker of the party. It is my sincere belief that we, in the Jan Awaaz, are all soldiers of the party. No doubt there is a need for a General to lead and steer the army of workers in the correct direction; still, he is also a soldier."

Ajit now paused to look at the huge crowd. "Let me begin," he said in a louder voice, "by saying that if The Right to Be Heard Act is the answer to Jan Awaaz, then the CCP has already conceded defeat." The crowd did not stop clapping for a full five minutes. Ajit continued in his normal tone.

"As you all must be aware, I had no intention whatsoever of forming a new party. Friends, the line taken by my respected peers in the BGP left you and me with little choice. I have said so in the past and reiterate again today, loudly and clearly for all to hear. Our philosophy is to put the nation first, then the party, and only then the individual.

"This sounds idealistic. When I say put the nation first, the question arises: Who is to do so? Do we do this as a people? If everybody in this crowd now takes an oath to put the nation first will it be enough? We can indeed take the oath but how would we execute our decision? Our aim must be to make it practically achievable. The way to that is to first feel as individuals, then think about it as individuals, and finally act as individuals. Even though we may be acting separately as individuals, our actions will add up to achieve the greater good. There is no real contradiction between individual human action and a collective human goal like welfare for all.

"Our ultimate goal is to create a just and prosperous society. Merely creating a 'just society' is not enough. In fact, many such societies in the past were very unjust to several sections of their population. It is only when we strive for prosperity that true social justice is realised. To attain this, what we need is not 'collective effort', what we need is individual action, brought together by a fair and transparent system. One pillar for this stands in the form of individual liberty and private property. Another is the rule of law. A third would a system of checks and balances in the way the government functions.

"I have been in what is called 'politics' for quite a long time now. In all these years, many things have changed, but some problems stubbornly refuse to go away. Thus, even today, we hear of atrocities based on caste, religion, gender and wealth. Atrocities on women, female infanticide and the like. And the one uninvited guest who refuses to go away is poverty. Even polio has been eradicated in India, but poverty clings to us like a piece of sticky dirt. Is this our fate? I think not!

"Friends, today I wish to initiate a movement that I hope will help us eradicate this scourge. We are a political party. But why are we in politics? In my time I have worn many hats – a sportsman, a model and an activist. I could have confined myself to my work, made money, done a bit of charity, sent a message through my writing and speeches and been content with that. Should I be content with that? The answer is a resounding 'no'. The answer is 'no' because there is more to life than a profession. Make no mistake, everybody must have a profession, and every profession is divine. But we should not stop with just that.

"Can we keep quiet when we see our fellow human beings suffer in silence? Can we keep quiet when, for no fault of their own, innocent people are subjected to cruelty in the name of caste, religion or ideology? Can we keep silence in the face of huge disparities in wealth? Wealth often earned by unfair means? The corrupt becoming richer while the hard workers continue to struggle?

"Again my answer is 'no'. We have to do something, and I am happy to announce that we, all of us gathered here, have already done that something. We have taken that first irrevocable step. We have taken up a cause on behalf of the public. That cause is the future of our nation, the well being of the generations to follow us. Fighting for a public cause –that is politics to me.

"A statesman once said that politics is the art of the possible. Mahatma Gandhi taught us that politics is a means to an end. He emphasised that if our means are faulty, then, however laudable our ends may be, they will be tainted. The living proof of the truth in what the Mahatma said can be seen in the kind of politics practiced in India and other counties in the region.

"Are we in politics for getting power? Remember that this is a legitimate end. Are we in politics to ensure that a coalition government we might have helped to form stays in power? Are we in politics because we like the power and the prestige that power confers upon us?

"Other people, normal politicians, political parties, might think so. I tell you that none of the questions I asked just now leads us to the answer. And that answer is 'TO CHANGE'. Challenge assumptions and change yourself first. You will then witness the change permeating society. I sincerely believe that you and I are in politics to achieve that change. Change in the attitudes of the people, change in their standard of living, change in the way they interact with each other. In a word, transformation!

"Our party is called Jan Awaaz. We champion the fact that everyone is equal, without the boundaries of caste, religion, region or language. Yet, the equality that we espouse is different from that of the others. We do not mistake uniformity for equality.

"Let me quote Dr. Ambedkar: 'My social philosophy is enshrined in the three words: liberty, equality and fraternity. I have not borrowed this from the French Revolution. My philosophy has roots in Buddhism. Unlimited liberty destroys equality, while absolute equality leaves no room for liberty. Fraternity or brotherhood is essential to preserve liberty and equality. Mere law and legislation cannot achieve what men and women do not believe and practice wholeheartedly.'

"We too believe in the equality that upholds the liberty of individuals, moderated by the fraternity between individuals and groups. When we say we consider everyone equal, we must first believe and practice this precept. Again, let me remind you, equality does not imply uniformity. Uniformity means that all of us should do the same thing - as in a military drill.

"Take a running race. Everyone starts at the beginning line and start to run after a whistle is blown. Everyone is equal in the sense that they are all at the start line and begin running at the same time. As the race begins, each one of them has the liberty of running as fast as they can. Different people will run at different speeds and usually only one will finish first. Yet, while running, the runners have to keep to their own track, implying fraternal relations with other competitors.

"Suppose a rule is made that the only goal is to reach first and you can run however you want. People will jump lanes and the strong and unscrupulous runners will block the way of others in order to reach the finish line first. Many of the blocked persons may actually be able to run faster, but will be unable to even finish, let alone win.

"Similarly, if a rule is made which says that since some persons may not have had a good breakfast that morning, the others should not overtake them even if they are able to. Another person suggests that since we believe in equality, just as everybody began together, so also everyone should finish together at the same time, without regard for the speed at which they can race. Would that be correct?

"We need all three –equality, liberty and fraternity. The concept of fraternity was defined pithily by the Tamil poet Thiruvalluvar two thousand years ago, when he outlined the concept of 'Opuravu'. *'The benevolent man should serve society seeking no return, for, how can the earth recompense the bounty of the rain-clouds?* Rajaji called this 'active social co-operation with the spirit of helpfulness behind it'.

"Real equality means that we are given the room, the liberty, to realise the full potential in all of us, whatever our caste, religion or social background. In the South, we have the shining example of a bus conductor who has become a superstar. Had society insisted that a bus conductor should only be a bus conductor for the rest of his life, we would have lost a cinema icon.

"Today, this confusion between equality and uniformity is at its highest. This confusion has prevented us from identifying the real problems, analysing them with a dispassionate mind and proposing real and practical solutions to those problems. To my mind, the biggest problem today is that there is too much of the usual kind of politics based on caste, religion and so on. And too much of politicking, that is, giving a political angle to every little thing. This has lead to a situation where every issue is so immersed in politics that rational and people friendly solutions are almost impossible to implement.

"Let us put ourselves back at the start line of politics. The first step to cleanse politics is to depoliticise economics. This is how we can ensure that all start at the starter's whistle. Let us not forget that some us can run faster than others. What we must not be deceived into believing is that economics is a zero-sum game. That is if one earns more, then that can be only at the cost of another's income. This may have been true in colonial times, when our freedoms were limited. This is not true at present.

"Today, it is possible for everyone to get richer. This has been made possible by advances in technology and in the methods of organisation. Economic policy and actions on the economic front should be taken on the merits of the solutions advanced and the practicality of the steps. We must take real action to ensure that the policies adopted by the government are translated into benefits for the people; both in the short term and the long term and for specific groups as well as for society at large.

"We must 'put an obligation on the state to plan the economic life of the people on lines which would lead to highest point of productivity without closing every avenue to private enterprise, and also provide for the equitable distribution of wealth,' said Dr. Ambedkar. The Government's role in such a plan would be to provide stability. Stability of policy, good governance, and rule of law. And to prevent, by transparent means, the exploitation of the weaker sections of society, by the rich and the strong.

"Look at the power shortages, astronomically high land and house prices, continuous inflation, shortage of essential goods and commodities. All these can be remedied by appropriate policies. Take power generation – it requires a long gestation period and a huge capital outlay. A practical policy would, in the first step, encourage private entrepreneurs to invest in power generation, allowing the government to purchase power at the cheapest rates. Once we build enough capacity, though this may take some years, we can also think of encouraging competition in the distribution of power. If you wonder whether this will work, you need to look no further than our telecom sector. When, about a decade ago, the government loosened controls, the sector bloomed. Even as late as in the year 2000, it was customary to ask, 'Do you have a phone?' Today, we ask, 'What is your mobile number?' Such has been the penetration of mobile phones.

"In sector after sector, this has held true. Competition drives down prices and pushes up quality. Poverty denotes absence of wealth, possessions, lack of goods and services, lack of achievement. We would like to emphasise that we want everyone to have everything. This can be achieved only if we free people to participate in the economic process. I use the word 'participate' deliberately. I could have used the word 'inclusion'. Inclusion implies exclusion –that some are not invited to the party. Participation implies that it is voluntary and that it is equal and that it is contributory. As I said at the beginning, we are all equal when we stand at the same start line.

"There is a Chinese saying: *Give a man a fish, you will feed him for one day; teach a man to fish and you feed him for life*. Our aim is to feed our masses for life, by educating them, by equipping them with world-class skills, by instilling self-confidence, by encouraging entrepreneurship, by discouraging monopolies and by creating a positive environment for growth tempered by equity.

"What we do not need are TV talk-shows, a host of so-called experts and their great debates. In purely economic terms, the solutions are known – what we do need is to adapt the solutions to the time and place and actually 'sell' them to our people. We need a government that gets down to work and implements the policy laid out in a practical and timely manner.

"To do this, we need leaders, dynamic leaders, the kind who speak out their minds and do not shun taking risks. The kind of leader who is unafraid of mingling with common people, who understands peoples' problems and who is capable of generating workable solutions. A good leader is one who treats a fever for its cause, not for its symptoms. A man of straw would be content to treat it with a painkiller. The fever will subside temporarily but come back once the effect of the tablet wears off. How many painkillers can we keep on eating and how many times are we going to think that all problems can be solved with quick, even if convenient, fixes?

"There are two kinds of leaders. One who pretends to lead but actually does only what his or her followers wants him/her to do. The late Ramakrishna Hegde, the former Chief Minister of Karnataka, likened them to Utsava Murthys, the idols that are taken about in processions. After the procession, their role too ends.

"The other kind is the one who leads out of conviction. This type of person works not for the applause of the crowd, but for real transformation. The yen for service to humanity marks the real leader like Sardar Patel, like Lok Nayak Jaya Prakash Narayan, Netaji Subhas Chandra Bose, Nehru, Dr. Ambedkar or Rajaji. An NTR, who stood up for Telugu pride, or an MGR who worked for the welfare of the masses in neighbouring TamilNadu.

"As I have emphasised, a real leader is also first and foremost a tireless worker. I want every one of you to be such a leader. I want a party of leaders, a nation of leaders. Real leaders, who strive to serve society and the nation. If we become such leaders, a party of such wonderful workers who really do not need to be 'led', then people will give us their wholehearted support.

"We have enough ideologies of all colours and stripes. What we need are ideas. Ideas, rather than mere ideology. We must sift between the good and the not-so-good ideas and drop the bad ones. We must choose the good ideas, the workable solutions, and use them to solve the real problems that people face. Let us leave dry ideologies behind and embrace good ideas, wherever they originate from. Let us all join hands to produce a real and better tomorrow for our people.

"People honour those who give, not those who take. The greatest happiness is not in wealth, or assets, but in seeking out and in serving others. This is what Swami Vivekananda meant when he urged the youth to serve 'Daridra Narayana'.

"The theme you must take up is: 'Make politics pure'. The first step to that is to depoliticise economics. This is necessary to give our people a fair chance to achieve the personal goals they have set for themselves and to root out poverty. Our aim is to create a just, prosperous and equitable society, enabling people to lead happy and fulfilling lives.

"In this huge effort, as I said at the beginning, I stand before you, not as a neta but as the first worker of the party."

Paresh was electrified. In his imagination, he saw a contented and prosperous nation. He also saw that he had the answer to the conundrum posed by Ishwar. The trick was to take a step however small and continue taking steps so that over a period of time a transformational solution is reached.

He had asked Divya if they could meet for a quick bite at a local restaurant. As of that morning, he had no idea how to resolve this dilemma. It had to be now or never. He drew a deep breath and squared his shoulders. As a recent practitioner of yoga, he had learned to perform without worrying too much about the outcome. He decided to make his pitch and leave the rest to God.

He need not have worried. Divya arrived punctually for lunch. Clearly, something was worrying her. He looked up from his plate of chicken biriyani only to find her looking at him. What he saw in her eyes set his pulse racing. He opened his mouth to speak, and just as quickly concluded that it was redundant. The language of her eyes was eloquent. He reached across and squeezed her hand.

"Will you?" was his simple question. At that moment, even that seemed long-winded. She simply nodded her head.

Even as learned analysts and political commentators pontificated on how impossible it would be for Ajit to enter into a coalition or to manage one even if he did, the common people of India delivered their judgement. The electorate turned up in large numbers. The subaltern strategy paid off big time. Jayashree Mandal delivered Uttar Pradesh, while the JA carried Bihar on its own steam. The large crowds that Ajit attracted kept his party men in line. Even Jagdiswar Singh privately acknowledged the Ajit wave. The JA won the elections with a thumping majority.

Padamji preferred the cool climate of London and the welcoming arms of Denise to seeing Ajit sworn in as PM. Strangely, press criticism was muted. 'Poor man' seemed to be their refrain. 'He needs rest after such an unexpected defeat.'

END